My Year With Sammy

Libby Sommer

My Year With Sammy

Thank you to Natasha Sommer for editing advice

My Year With Sammy
ISBN 978 1 76041 064 3
Copyright © text Libby Sommer 2015
Cover painting: Erika Sommer

First published 2015 by
GINNINDERRA PRESS
PO Box 3461 Port Adelaide 5015
www.ginninderrapress.com.au

Contents

Part One

1

Sammy said she doesn't like kisses. No kisses and no hugs. She would roll on the floor and wrestle with and jump on top of her dog in between the uncontrollable storms full of accusations that swept us all up like a tsunami above her childhood. I wasn't surprised one day when I saw her lying on the new couch, in the new house, beside her brother, her newly adopted cat, one of a pair, asleep on her stomach, the blue brother, who she called Mister Sphinx.

She is a girl of many moods; she says things like, I don't remember. She told me she'd been on a school excursion, she didn't know where, and I believed her. She said she'd caught swimmer crabs and scorpions but she'd let them all go.

2

At the sea pool, Sammy digs her toes into the grass, face down on her striped beach towel.

Are you okay, Princess? I ask.

She says, Yes, Mummy Number Two.

Bits of dirt collect in the hollows beneath her ankles. Every time she sighs, another few twigs collect there. She's still small enough to lie beside me and use my shade, although we're up on the grass under a tree, near the sand of the beach. There, next to me, she is in hiding; protected by the presence of my largeness. But if she lifts her head and looks over her shoulder, she can see the water of the ocean.

It is mid-September. Further up the grassy slope, a group of bare-chested young men in boxer swimmers sit cradling cold beers or glasses of red wine from a cask, before they run along the wooden perimeter of the pool and jump into the water that is outside the shark net, then clamber back up the netting to leap in again. They don't bother us.

She is beside me now, my daughter's child, and I acknowledge this, sometimes stroking her head with the palm of my hand. I am aware of the thinness of her body, like when she raced up the steps and in my front door. I caught her on the way through and hugged her little body close and kissed her on the cheek and told her how much I'd missed her. She gave a smile. The memory of this embrace is the memory of catching her in full flight. I am strong and nuggety and Sammy is long-limbed and slight of build, constructed to climb and swing from tree branches with monkey-like agility. Her shoulders are unfleshed and rounded, the firm shoulders of a high-wire acrobat, and, for this, she is admired by her brother when he stands below a tree in readiness to help her when her foot is stuck between the trunk and a high branch, his blue school shirt hanging loose over his grey shorts. With her shoe stuck in the tree, Sammy takes the shape of a gymnast, a renegade one – no professional – with her brown hair hanging loose and free.

Sammy is very beautiful, but who wouldn't say that? She has teeth that become prominent when she laughs – an open-mouthed generous laugh that comes from deep in her solar plexus. Her teeth capture that laugh and encircle it like a precious gift, unwrap it after a moment into a broad smile. Her softness is significant – her soft hair, thick, mid-brown, full of character; and the softness of her shoulders. She often beautifies herself, lipstick if she can find some, green fingernails, glitter-emerald toenails. There is a delicate boniness to her face: she is cheekbones and eyes and mouth. But her face is set in place by sheer force of will, by a stubborn internal command. She's not compliant. She doesn't let me kid myself that she'll do what I ask. I'm not her mother, after all.

Sammy brushes the dirt off her towel, rests her head on her arms. She doesn't say anything to me, but she knows I am here, a particle of her thoughts. My worrying brain thinks, thinks, and free falls across the spring fragrances that connect us. She trails behind me; she's unpredictable. Her eyes absorb the bright blue or the pale grey of the morning sky – whatever the time of day – repelling darkness, translucent. Sammy is not the clearly drawn profile of a typical eight-year-old girl; she is not transparent.

She is no stranger to beaches, is not afraid of the water. My mouth closes in the perilous air. I fill with worry and it catches in my throat. There is nothing that I can say or do. I imagine a short hastily written email: I am here if you need me. Her mother knows that.

Soon Sammy will go for another swim. To prepare myself, so I will not spend the whole time worrying, I see in my mind in precise detail Sammy swimming across the ocean pool, one paddle after the next, swimming past surfboards, past the seagulls; she swims the way gulls fly, consistently, steadily, across the vast expanse. She strokes towards the shore with an uneven rhythm in the calm water. She swims very close to the beach. I can see her, the determined chin and the pursed lips. Just beyond the breakers, her legs fall beneath her, and she walks upright through the waves. Down on the beach, she shakes the water from her arms, from her legs, and with a swift shaking of her head, she whips her hair to the sides and walks to where I am on the grass, spraying me with water.

I stop stroking her hair, and – there – she notices me again, in my own particular body, in her floral swimsuit a pattern similar to mine. She pushes her fingers into the dirt at her sides, and it makes them brown. She is a daredevil.

Watch me! she says. I'm going for a dip.

And she lifts herself from the towel in one sideways, swift action. She is halfway to the water. I sit up and stretch my spine to watch. She hits the water and all her movements slow. She ducks her head under the sea, her whole body now submerged beneath the surface. Her hands pull through the water, her feet kicking wildly. She emerges, turns on to her back, floats there with only her small face exposed, struggling to keep her legs stretched out, rather than sinking down beneath her. The water keeps lifting her and she drifts my way.

And I watch. If I do not watch, what will become of her?

3

I thought you'd be pleased to know, my daughter says, that after ski school, Sammy didn't throw her usual tantrum. Instead, she slammed down her skis in the snow and screamed, I just want to do what I want to do. At least she's using words now to express herself.

My daughter rises to her feet – hire-wire acrobat, juggler, contortionist, bile-swallower.

I look across to Sammy, whose legs are stretched out in front of her, while her toenails dry. They've been painted a bright emerald green. She is courageous with her choices and never allows us to forget that she's the one who'll be doing the choosing. She is so much in control. She's sitting silent in a black massage chair at the beauty salon, her toes wedged apart by one of those rubbery separator things, her own person. Her zip-up black boots stand beside the big chair, her thongs on her lap ready to wear home. We wait, her mother, her brother and me. Through the manicures and pedicures all around, she sits quietly on the chair, all on her own. She takes it all in to her serious eight-year-old mind, her face impassive, not looking our way.

Light from the overhead tear-drop chandelier bounces from ceiling to wall. With its curved mirrors and velvet-covered chaise longue, it's as inviting as a woman's boudoir. A glittering effect for a plain shop on the corner of an arcade, newly painted mushroom pink, to soothe the mind.

What does it cost to have Sammy's nails done? I ask my daughter.

Only ten dollars. She doesn't let me cut her toenails.

Rows of women along the walls on either side their feet relaxing in foot spas, fingers claw-like in bowls of water, heads bent over fashion magazines, their spines massaged up and down by the movement within their chairs. Across the black and white tiles of the floor, Sammy's ten-year-old brother James reclines on a couch in the reception area. He's writing in his school journal:

> My mother, Madelaine Rebecca, works as a web designer and saves dollars to pay the rent. She was doing the same work before the split up with my dad, but now she has to work every day, with no days off. My father, Bradley James, is out cycling in the park, laughing and joking around with his girlfriend, Pat. She is pretty, like Mummy. Mummy has long golden hair and soft knitted tops and tight straight jeans. Her toe nails are painted too. Her hair hangs loose and curly to her shoulders, like Alice in Wonderland.

He looks up at his mother. Did Sammy have a massage in the chair?

Don't mention massage in front of her, Madelaine hisses, or she'll want one.

James sinks back into the couch. I'm dying from sugar overload, he sighs.

You didn't let him have a Coke did you, Mum?

He told me you let him have large slushies.

No, James interrupts. I said Dad lets me have a large one.

Wall to wall, women lean back transfixed, while on low stools in front or beside them, uniformed Asian women, like exotic air hostesses with pink blouses buttoned to the neck, remove dead skin from cracked heels and bitten cuticles. They glance up when someone passes by but continue, protected by latex gloves, to massage watery cream into legs and hands. From the array of nail polishes at the side of the room, masked women apply false nails with designs of hearts or stripes or spots, or even diamond studs.

Choose a colour, someone calls out as another customer walks in.

4

When Sammy was three-and-a-half, the counsellor had made a 'diagnosis': emotional immaturity. My daughter's eyes filled with tears when she told me the preschool advised that some outside help was the answer. Sammy needs to learn to manage her emotions, the counsellor said. The school will monitor her behaviour.

As my daughter talked, I looked into her pale tired face, the latest outbreak of stress highlighted by the morning sun: the angry rash and the outbreak of pimples. I put my arms around her. But Sammy's only three, I said. I'm still learning to manage my emotions.

It's a conspiracy, Mum, she said. No one tells you. No one tells you how hard it all is.

Madelaine liked to share these things. Through the summer days we talked together in the brightly lit back room of her house on the lower north shore, a hot space cooled by a ceiling fan, where I helped bring the clothes in off the line and fold and sort the washing. She'd say things like Put your hair up, Mum. Wear a skirt. Trousers are far too hot in this weather. You can borrow something of mine.

Whenever we finished folding the cotton shorts and tops and we'd grouped all the socks in pairs, she would carry the individual piles into the bedrooms. She'd beckon me to follow, talking still as she opened the cupboards and drawers. When we'd brought the last load in off the clothesline and out of the dryer and the floor was totally clear – you could even see the ceramic tiles again – we'd take a break. Then she'd offer me a cup of tea, setting the mugs on the bench as the kettle boiled, and we'd share one of her freshly baked golden Anzac cookies.

In a corner of the room, near the window, she stored her large wooden easel, a row of completed paintings lined up on the floor on either side of it. An exhibition date loomed. Among the canvases was a picture of a woman wading through chest-deep water with a small child strapped to her back. In another, a mother looked into the middle distance as she breastfed her baby. I noticed the card my daughter had written for the catalogue: *The loneliness and the isolation of motherhood.*

Madelaine talked to me in random declarative sentences. Sometimes, her stories about the children made me laugh. It's so funny, Mum, she said, since Sammy was put in the group with a green hat at kindy, and because all the other members of her group are boys, Sammy's been saying she's a boy. When someone throws a ball towards her, she'll shout, Watch out for my nuts.

Madelaine called her daughter Sammy, rather than Samantha. Most of Sammy's friends were boys. I'd see her in the park impressing the other kids with what height she could jump from, with just how fearless she was. When older boys asked her name, she'd lift her head and say, I'm Sammy. They'd join in as she led packs of children in a charge up the hill and into the dark of the bushes.

This is how things were. Each week when I picked Sammy up from preschool I waited as she prepared to slide down the Fireman's Pole in the play area. Then it was one more swing, one more balance along the brick ledge or one of the other long rituals she had to perform – opening the gates for the parents and children to go through, the struggle with the heavy doors – I can do it! The endless goodbyes to her friends, the special path she had to run around before getting to the front gate, the walking backwards to the car.

The routine was to pick her up from kindy and then drive to the big school to get James. After I'd sign the book with the pick-up time I'd find Sammy on the fireman's pole with her little brown legs and delicate hands wrapped around the steel post. I'd reach up towards her on the high platform but she'd scowl at me. Don't help me. She'd turn her head and lean towards the pole, clamping her legs even tighter around it. I don't need you.

The thing was, I was battling a deadline to get up to James – his first year at school. James has soft blond hair and sensitive eyes. One day, when we arrived late, he thought no one was coming. One of the other parents was consoling him. So I couldn't be late.

Sometimes, the only thing to do was drag Sammy off the swing or the fireman's pole and take her kicking and screaming out the door. Help me, someone! she'd call out. Everyone turned around to look. She'd grab onto any posts or trees within her reach and hang on as tight as she could. I had to use all my strength to get her out of there – into the car, out of the car, up to the school.

Wilful. That's a better word for Sammy.

I've done my bit, said a reluctant grandmother I know. I'm not interested in doing it all again, said another woman. I take an anti-inflammatory on the day I'm due to have the grandchildren, even before I get the backache, she said.

One of the kindy mothers asked me if Sammy was looking forward to starting school next year. I don't know, I said. I'll have to ask her. When I asked Sammy the question, she screwed up her face as if in pain.

Why, darling? Why not?

She pretended to cry. I'm a bit bad, she said. She looked up at me with her hazel eyes, flecked with gold and contorted her face again. Time out, she said. The naughty corner.

You know how to be a good girl, I said, and kissed her on the forehead.

Sammy likes a bit of rough and tumble, I said to a friend. Jokingly, I added, Sometimes I wonder if she'll end up being one of those butch girls with short spiky hair riding a motorbike.

Don't be so silly. She's a free spirit, that's all.

A free spirit. That's how Madelaine's father described Madelaine in his father-of-the-bride speech. Past tense.

The wedding had been an interfaith ceremony. They were both proud of their religious heritage. Husband and wife stood under a Jewish chuppah and took their marriage vows under the traditional canopy. Madelaine wanted the customary Jewish ritual, so her new husband stamped on a glass wrapped in white linen. A celebrant crossed two waxen floral crowns over their heads in the usual Greek Orthodox manner.

I'm wondering what will happen when Sammy goes to school next year, my daughter said as she shuffled the order of paintings. Her dad says she's three going on thirteen. He reckons if she's like this now, what's she going to be like as a teenager? He thinks she's planning to take control of the whole family.

The woman in me then that folded and sorted, the part of me that assumed a distinct role in my daughter's mind — that woman was the mother she gave accounts to of the problems at home. She said the counsellor told them that different ideas about discipline could polarise a couple. Madelaine didn't talk to me about her love for her husband. He is the one between the sentences, the middle-class professional, the one who walked in and out of the house, furious: shit mother. Shit mother. Shit wife. Shit homemaker.

I know you don't like hearing these things, Mum — and she meant, I knew it, that his violent outbursts were all her fault.

He's the one who needs to learn to manage his emotions, I said.

When I first met him, my daughter said, I was thinking, he's not the sort of man I usually go for, a man so unsure of himself. I wasn't thinking, this is someone lacking in self-control, someone who does not understand.

She talked as if it was a new discovery, the storms of abuse that chipped away at her, this flaw deep within the heart of a man.

There's nothing we can do, Madelaine's father said to me. It's up to her. Probably best if you stay on your side of the Harbour Bridge.

Helpless. That's the word.

The next week, when I took the children to the park after school, that park where men play boules on the other side of the fence, James ran over to the wooden train and climbed up to the roof. He prepared for take-off. I hurried over. Be careful, I yelled hopelessly into the wind. He landed safely in the sand. Don't watch! my daughter would say. It's not so bad if you don't watch.

Sammy ordered me to pick up sticks to make a big fire for the train's engine before climbing up the slippery dip. Her brother slid down through her legs. She dangled dangerously from the top. I rushed over. She brushed me aside. She had that look in her eyes that I knew so well – her face monkey-like, the deep grooves of determination between her eyebrows and around her mouth, queen of her realm on top of the slippery dip.

The wind picked up and blew through the sandpit as the last of the afternoon light bounced off the leaves of the Moreton Bay figs. It's the end of a long week, I apologised to one of the mothers as Sammy screamed loudly at the woman's son who'd been telling Sammy that she is very naughty.

I'm not a nawty girl! she shouted at him.

The two children sat high up on the metal platform of the slippery dip yelling back and forth at each other. The boy wore a woollen beanie and his eyes were bright and round, the green of the irises scattered with brown dots like currants in an Anzac cookie. They stared at each other, the way people do after fighting-words are spoken, one on the attack, and the other on the defensive.

The little boy said, very loudly, You *are* a naughty girl, with what I decided was malice.

I saw two missing teeth. I asked him to stop saying Sammy was naughty because it upset her. It's the end of a long week, I apologised to the boy's mother. She's overtired.

The woman turned to her friend and said, Looks like the beginning of a long weekend. She told her son to go and sit on the park bench to have some time out on the chair.

Shoulders slumped, his eyes downcast, the boy dragged his feet through the sand and went to sit on the bench.

Overhead, bunches of puffy clouds drifted across the sky to reveal a pale sun. I turned my worrying mind away from the children and zipped my jacket up before walking across to the chair.

I sat down heavily, next to the little boy.

5

Sammy takes the little bunch of leaves into her hand. I love them, she says.

She might paste them with sticky tape on to that big cardboard box her mother gave her yesterday. A big empty box. There's almost nothing she likes better than to cut holes into a box for eyes, arms and legs. Yesterday she looked like a tortoise with the box on her back and her arms and legs sticking out of its holes.

So she's got the cluster of leaves in her tiny, delicate hands. The emerald green of her nails is so much brighter than the pale grey green of the dead leaves. Firstly, she looks into the leaves, examines them closely, runs her thumb and forefinger along their length; is able to discern the moisture still in the almost dead leaf. She turns them over. Looks where each leaf in the group of three, is joined to the other.

Thanks, she says. Thanks for the present. Where's the sticky tape?

Here, in this drawer, Sammy's mother says as she pulls out the black container from the drawer of her desk, on top of which is her laptop and a pile of bills to be paid.

The desk sits beside the new set of drawers that she purchased last week from Ikea. Her container of tools in a plastic sleeve sits on the top of the white melamine. She'd announced proudly on Facebook that she'd built a chest of drawers.

With the sticky tape in hand, Sammy secures the bunch of dead leaves to her cardboard tortoise. She's decorating the hard shell of the animal's back. On second thoughts, she decides to separate each of the three leaves and arrange them differently. The box has now become a huge rectangular face. The holes for the tortoise's arms are now eye sockets. She decides to stick a long skinny leaf above each eye and turns them into eyebrows.

The third leaf becomes a moustache. She climbs into the box from on top of the couch, one leg at a time until the length of her body is upright, covered in cardboard. She presses her face against the eye holes and peers out. Look at me, she doesn't say.

But her mother senses that she needs to turn round, and she sees the funny cardboard face with dead leaves as eyebrows.

I imagine a hastily scrawled note:

Dear Mummy Two,

Mummy made me write this letter to say thanks so much for the bunch of dead leaves. It's really made me appreciate that the simple things in life can be better than all those expensive games and things in the shops. Mummy gave me the empty box and you gave me something right out of left field that I could use to add character. If it wasn't for you, the big rectangular face would have no eyebrows and no moustache. So thanks, Mummy Two, for helping to stimulate my imagination. Mummy told me to say that bit. If it wasn't for you and for my darling mummy, I would have stayed watching television all afternoon and into the night. Instead, I've created a unique creature. Sometimes I lie on my back with the box covering my body and with only my arms and legs sticking out, just like a tortoise with a shell trapped on its back. Mummy says I have a great imagination. Did you see my new painting on one of mummy's old huge canvases? She let me paint right over the top of her flower.

6

It wasn't Bondi. I knew that. But it had rolling, magnificent waves, and there was a row of Norfolk Island palms, and the beach was bordered with park lands dotted with thatched-roof beach shelters. On the slope, a section was contoured into a children's playground, which filled each summer with groups of barbecuing families – do-it-yourself matchless hot plates – the aquamarine of the sea, the various shades of green of the leaves, and the upright rigidity, the solid, bright azure blue of the parking meters, the same blue as the buses that belched up the hill.

All this seemed idyllic; but the daily routine was no walk on the beach. Madelaine said that life with Sammy was like living with a loose cannon. She'd stopped caring what the other mothers at the school thought, with their perfect children. And she didn't appreciate being told by Sammy's other grandmother how she should parent Sammy. At the winter Friday night netball game, too, especially there, Madelaine knew Sammy would most likely have a meltdown – she'd lie by the court all wrapped up in her furry coat and say she felt sick; or be reprimanded by the coach for cartwheeling across the court; or sob hysterically that she couldn't play centre and had never ever played centre. Random tantrums that brought her mother to tears of frustration.

But the other parents didn't consider these things. They had their own children to worry about. If one of the girls got hurt during the match, somebody ran for the ice packs, and Madelaine and all the other parents would rush over to help before sending another child on as a replacement.

When the game finished, Sammy showed me her purple hands and spread her palms up – See, Mummy Two, see how cold I am, she said, and touched her hands to mine.

It's true that Sammy called me Mummy Two. She took to that name.

She said she liked saying the words. Mummy One and Mummy Two, she'd laugh as Madelaine and I stood side by side watching James play football. I wasn't Granny or Nana, and that was fine. They called the other grandmother Nana.

I remember when James told me that Nana had set the house on fire at Dad's. James wanted to warn me not to heat the kettle on the stove. Nana put the kettle on the hot plates to make a cup of tea and it caught alight. When Sammy heard Nana call out 'Fire!' she'd come running into the kitchen. Sammy used her hands to show me the height of the flames. I expected to see a little fire, she told me, using her thumb and forefinger to illustrate. When I saw how big it was, I wasn't frightened. I'm not scared of anything, she said, shaking her head.

James said that Nana threw water from the sink on to the flames, but the fire ruined the stove. Nana should have smothered it with a woollen blanket, he said.

Maybe she didn't want to waste time looking for a blanket, I said. What did Dad do?

He went into his room and banged his head against the wall.

The week of the match, on my school pickup afternoon, I waited by the brick wall of the assembly hall. I could see Sammy when she ambled down the steps from her classroom. She knew I was there, but she wouldn't look at me. I waved my arms at her, as if waving a jet in for landing. She dumped her school bag at my feet with a thud. I hugged her thin body before she escaped my grasp; desperate to run over to the climbing tower.

Can I have a play? she called back over her shoulder.

She loved the playground. Climbing and swinging from the bars was her passion – an ongoing, intensely pursued passion, an accumulation of energy released, in contrast with the constraints of the classroom. School, of course, had rules. Rules were what human beings lived by, rather than acting freely according to one's nature.

School was something else for Sammy. It was loathsome, bewildering, non-inclusive. It showed itself always as humiliation. Under its influence, it chipped away at her confidence, with some kind of destructive mechanism preset and ticking. We all knew it. You walked over to her at school of an afternoon to pick her up, and – bam! She shot off like a bullet. Learning difficulties – a natural target for school bullies. I don't cry, she'd say. I'm tough.

Summer school holidays were different; out amidst nature on the beach or in the park. Summer was loved, panoramic, calming. In its warmth, she ran along the beach, with some kind of stress-release device reset and ticking.

But today she was on top of the play equipment at school and wouldn't come down. She leaned back on the steel rods on top of the monkey bars as we waited for her brother. She rubbed the red and blistering skin of her palms, and spat on to the throbbing pads before swinging across the bars again, her palms cooled by her own saliva.

In the playground, I watched as James and a friend threw each other's school bags over the bannister from the platform above the exterior stairs, where the new classroom block had been built with its noisy steel steps. Sometimes, a boy below would grab the bag and run around the building and throw it in one of the big rubbish bins and close the lid.

At the bottom of the steps, James called out to me, Can Jack come over for a play date?

Sure. I crossed the playground. But we'll have to ask his mum. Where is she?

My dad's here, Jack said. He pointed to a group of adults waiting outside the library. I'll ask him.

The two boys ran off.

James said he didn't like playing with his sister, that it always ended up with her screaming or hitting him. I asked James if she was like that at their dad's.

Sammy plays up as much for Dad as she does for Mum, he said. She fights with everyone. With Dad and with Nana. But not in front of Pat. She never throws a tantrum in front of Pat. Never, he added in an exasperated voice.

I looked over to Sammy hanging like a bat from the monkey bars. It was time to get the children home. Jack's dad had said, Not today. No play date today. So James yelled out impatiently to his sister, If you don't come down right now, no television for the whole week.

Every time, it was the same struggle. I'll handle it, I said to James. I called up to Sammy, I've got a special treat in the car.

What? she said. What is it?

When she finally climbed down, I swung her bag on to my shoulder and crossed the asphalt to the back gate.

Can we go for a swim? pleaded Sammy. Please. Please.

Using my body like a shepherd with his sheep, I herded the two children towards the pedestrian crossing. Not today, I said to Sammy. Maybe next time. I reached for her hand, but knew she wouldn't let me hold it to cross the road. Your nails look beautiful, Sammy. What a lovely tangerine colour.

She stretched her hands out in front of her to examine her long and slender fingers. I want to go for a swim, she said.

Who painted your fingernails?

Pat. Pat…ricia.

Oh. Pat? You mean Daddy's friend?

Sammy ran down the footpath towards the car. I could see the black soles of her retreating shoes and hear the slap slap sound as she raced down the hill. James ran ahead to beat his sister to the car.

The sky was thick with grey. The smell of rain in the air, although the days were lengthening into summer. The two cats would be waiting for us at the front door. They went off during the day in and out of the kitchen window to steal peacock feathers from next door's collection, or to climb on the roof of the town houses or to explore in the bushes. They had been home all alone, after all, and they liked to be cuddled and stroked. They slept on the children's beds, Mister Sphinx with Sammy, and Lulu with James. Sometimes the two children and the two cats slept all together on the double bed with Madelaine. All squashed in close to each other in the big bed.

This is how things were.

7

Outside is the sound of water pelting down, a hose spraying, all over the place. The flow seems to stop in mid-direction, fall, funnel. Sammy is circling it in the air, then, after a long pause, it's falling all over Sammy's head and it soaks her hair and her school dress. She doesn't care.

She's told me she's not afraid of anything. But I know she's scared of the dark. Her brother said she leaves the light on all night in the room they share at their father's house. James complains he has to lie turned toward the wall. Sammy says it's the same wherever she sleeps; she likes to have the light on. It's the same thing at Mum's – a buzzy fly or a mosquito in the middle of the night, in rooms with screens on the windows and curtains over the blinds. Sammy needs three things on the table next to the bed: a fly swatter – one of those plastic ones or a rolled-up newspaper; cream to put on in case you get bitten; and some spray. There shouldn't be a way for spiders and insects to get in, she said. But they do get in. And they never fly out. They never find their way out.

In those early years at primary school, Madelaine said that Sammy, when finally asleep, was a deep sleeper, curled around a soft toy, her eyelashes flickering. Sammy said she dreamt about pigs, her favourites, and that she had a pet pig living in the backyard. She mostly slept through the night, through thunder, through storms, and therefore her mother thought she could tell her about the discovery of a vaccine for mosquitoes that could stop the spread of dengue fever. She knew science was Sammy's favourite subject at school, and she thought her daughter would want to know about the new research.

But what if a mosquito or a fly gets in my room? Sammy asked her mother.

They don't get in your room, Sammy.

But what if they do?

They can't get in.

How do you know? Or a cockroach?

There aren't any cockroaches here.

There are cockroaches, Sammy said. She pointed at the ceiling. See. There's a fly and you said there aren't any flies.

Oh, such a funny girl. Such a muffin.

8

Sammy has promised that as soon as she's finished playing with the hose, she'll do her homework. She steps out of her wet school dress and wraps a blanket around herself then sinks on to the couch and picks up the TV remote. I tell her that Mummy said she has to do the special homework on the computer before the television goes on

James, busy on his iPod touch, is beside his sister, wearing his blue school shirt and grey shorts, his maroon Sea Eagles cap with the weather-beaten brim turned backwards. The other grandmother has discovered a special reading program for Sammy to do on the internet. James had told me that when Nana wanted to show their grandfather how well Sammy's going on the program, Sammy wouldn't do the spelling words in front of him.

James said Nana started up with the counting and threatening. His eyes had filled with tears at the memory of it all.

Nana should know better, I said. You can't force Sammy to do things. So what happened?

Sammy went into her room and shut the door.

Stretched out on the lounge now, Sammy points the remote at the TV screen. I remind her there's to be no television until she's done Nana's special computer lesson.

I know that, Sammy says. You don't have to tell me. I don't feel like doing it.

I often don't feel like doing things, I say. I didn't feel like going shopping for tonight's dinner, but I still did it.

She plugs her ears with her fingers. I just don't feel like it.

Madelaine had made it clear to me, no TV till Nana's program is done.

Don't turn the television on, I warn Sammy.

After a brief silence, she gets up and kicks off her wet shoes. She hurries off to find her iPod touch. And then she is slouched on the couch next to her brother, just out of my reach.

9

I breathe in the smell of jasmine and see glimpses of crimson bougainvillea through the gap in the sliding window as Mister Sphinx and Lulu climb in on to the granite bench top that separates the dining area and the kitchen. When the two cats re-enter the town house at the end of the day, I feed them with half a scoop each of dry cat food poured into silver bowls. The cats are trained to come in at dusk, and all day they are out looking for prey, primed for combat – in case they find a bird or a lizard, or any other small creature.

Six o'clock, and I serve up the kids' dinner; their mother is still at the gym. All of us see it at the same time – Mister Sphinx and Lulu tormenting a squirmy thing under the black rubber front doormat. The mat is made up of a pattern of holes. When a cockroach is trapped between the ground and its rubbery grasp, a cat can remove its shell.

Sammy jumps up from the table and screams. There's a cockroach! She runs up the stairs to her bedroom, her blanket trailing on the steps.

The cockroach gets stuck at first by the pressure of the mat on its back. A very heavy, weighted down sensation. The cat peers, his claws out and erect, like a snow leopard preparing to attack. The cockroach holds itself together, gathering strength and wondering how to proceed now that it's on its back. After a couple of seconds, it comes to an important decision and begins to do what it can, to struggle and turn itself over. It continues this last ditch effort as the cat's claw lashes out, until weariness sets in for the cockroach. Then it takes a rest and tries again to turn over. At each interval, a cat's claw removes more of its shell, exposing its naked torso. The cockroach lies there, and I feel its helplessness.

At that moment, James and I see his grandfather, a chair under each arm, step through the puddles of water and walk toward the open door.

He's come to deliver some more chairs. He peers at the white object caught between the holes of the mat. He declares it dead – kicks the remains into the grass – walks in across the white tiles, leaving behind a muddy footprint. He says, I hope I won't get into trouble.

I say, She's not like that. But don't worry, I'll clean the tiles.

He places the chairs around the dining table and moves back towards the front door. I bought that mat, he says proudly. But I have to go. She-who-must-be-obeyed is waiting in the car.

I've never heard him refer to her like that. Maybe James hasn't either, because I hear him say, Nana? Do you mean Nana?

Yep, I'd better go, he says.

I tell the children to come back to the table for dinner. Their mother hurries in as we start eating, in her lycra tights and singlet, her hair caught up in a bun. She throws down her gym bag, her face beaded with sweat; it glints like freshly watered glass. In that moment, she stands uncharacteristically upright, the tats down the nape of her neck startling in their pattern of stars. She looks less like a mother than a warrior ready for battle.

She walks up to the children and kisses them on the head. Something smells good, she says. She tells Sammy not to stuff her mouth with the pasta, she'll choke, but it makes no difference.

Sammy's cheeks bulge and distend. She's cramming the pasta in – single-minded as a missile headed for home.

10

Look at that, Madelaine whispers. This is what I want to talk to you about. See what she can be like? Madelaine nods towards Sammy at the kitchen bench and says something like sweet, sweet, sweet.

It is Monday evening, and Sammy is preparing dessert for us all. She calls out to me, How many strawberries do you want, Mummy Two? My Mummy wants just one.

Just one for me too, I say.

We sit on the newly delivered chairs in the dining room between the kitchenette and the lounge. We're diagonally opposite the settee where James is settled in with his iPod.

Mummy, Sammy calls out, do you want your strawberry cut into little pieces?

Yes, please.

Do you want yours chopped up, Mummy Two? Sammy asks.

Yes, I'll have the same.

Do you want a small bowl with ice cream and chocolate and the strawberry?

A large bowl for me, James calls out from the other room. I want the biggest serving. He gets up off the couch and hurries to the kitchen. He pulls out a big dish and places it next to the chopping board where Sammy is cutting up the strawberries.

Be careful of your fingers, Sammy, I say.

James takes the knife from his sister.

Let her do it, his mother says. Madelaine moves her chair closer to mine and lowers her voice. I want to tell you about the boy from next door, she says. There – on the other side of that wall. She points to the lounge room, where the divan is alongside the wall.

If I don't focus my eyes, my daughter's fingers appear to push against the lounge room wall, it is so imposing, so overbearing.

I say, Yes, I know where he lives.

She says, Good. I want to tell you what happened. You can talk about what I say or you can forget all about it. The boy who lives next door to us, she says, he's the one, the neighbour. That boy used to hang around here all the time, you remember? So, all of a sudden, he was knocking at the door again. The kids were watching TV and it was near dusk. From this chair, this same one, I saw the boy, walking up the pathway in camouflage shirt and pants, with a ball under his arm. He's tall now with olive skin and brown hair, all the colours of the front foliage and, I tell you, my first thought was a tree shifting. But he came to the door and bounced his basketball against the rubber mat. He asked if James and Sammy wanted to come outside and play.

Why had James stopped playing with him? I ask.

Because he's a bully.

Did they want to go with him?

Yes, and I was grateful they'd be out in the fresh air. I thought at the time, it's good to get them into the backyard. They need to run around. Although it always surprises me that the boy is so keen to include Sammy. She's just a little girl, after all. I stayed where I was, in this room working at my desk, until James staggered back in without saying a word. He was clutching at his throat and gasping for air.

So what happened?

James turned the tap on in the kitchen and put his mouth to the water, used his hand as a cup, and gagged at the same time. He said Sammy had tried to choke him. His sister nearly killed him.

Where is she? I asked him, but I thought I'd seen her running up the stairs.

When I went up to her room, it looked as if someone had ransacked the place, so much stuff spread across the carpet. It didn't look like anyone slept there, the mattress devoid of sheets, blankets or pillows, only a red heart-shaped cushion against the white painted wood of the bedhead. All the cats' playthings were spread across the floor; the spiral cat house draped with dangling strings; a cardboard box with a soft rug inside set up as a bed for the cats; a sign stuck to the door: No entry, cats only. Sammy mostly sleeps in my bed these days. But there was no sign of her anywhere.

It's not okay for her to hurt her brother, I put in.

I know that, my daughter says. I don't need you to tell me. Anyway, Sammy said later that James had taken aim, and then thrown the ball at her head.

It was only a soft throw, James pipes up from the sofa where he's waiting for his dessert.

You're lying, Sammy calls out from the kitchen.

I don't lie, James says. I threw the ball softly. You know that.

What did you expect? his mother says. You know she's going to retaliate if you do something like that.

But she didn't have to nearly kill me. I couldn't breathe.

She knows she did wrong.

Did you punish her? I ask.

They were both in the wrong, my daughter says.

Sammy brings a bowl over to the table and places it in front of her mother and then one for me. Here you go, she says. There's one extra big strawberry for Mummy. Can you see it? She searches through her mother's serving of melted ice cream and then my dish to check where the special strawberry has gone.

James returns to the table after picking up his plate from the kitchen. He sits back down. I said I didn't want my strawberries cut up, he says.

The very big strawberry is the one I'm talking about, Sammy says. It's a special one for Mummy. Where is it? Has someone eaten it?

When the kids are back on the couch in front of the TV, Madelaine continues with the story. She says James was still on the settee when the boy came back to the open doorway. He called out, Are you okay, James?

James kept playing on his iPod and didn't look up. Yes, he said.

The boy sat beside him on the divan and watched James play a game. On the desk was a small flat calculator, a Skype phone, a stapler, the cordless telephone handset, a mat and an empty coffee mug.

The boy said, So what are you doing? Can I have a turn?

No. I'm playing.

Can I be next?

It'll take me a long time to finish this.

No, it won't, the boy said. He sniffed inwards with an involuntary snort and moved closer on the couch. You're nearly at the end, he said. I can wait. Just finish that bit and then it's my turn.

They were still in the lounge room and he was reaching for a cat and setting the animal on his lap. He stroked down the cat's fur.

Where's Sammy's iPod? the boy asked. Is it down here somewhere? He placed the cat on the floor, the cat's hind legs in one hand and his chest in the other, and went over to the desk. He picked up the stapler and pointed it at James. You've got something on your head, he said. It's a cockroach.

James said, Yeah. Sure.

It's true. He set the stapler down and came towards James. He was a year older, with an older boy's swagger, only just aware of his power. His eyes were narrow slits when he smirked; they were dark in his face, and he looked out from beneath hooded lids.

James jumped up. Is there anything on my head? he asked me.

It's nothing, darling, I said. Just a leaf.

He lifted his hand and brushed it from his hair. He said in a gruff voice to the boy, Cut it out.

What? What have I done?

A little later there was a knock and the mother of the boy stood in the doorway. Is Mummy home? she asked James.

Here I am, I called out from the kitchen.

Sorry, said the mother. I didn't know he was in here.

It's okay. They were playing outside until a few minutes ago.

The boy and Sammy were now huddled together on the steps that led to her room, concentrating on Sammy's iPod. He had his arm around her shoulder.

Say goodbye, said the boy's mother.

I looked up to see the boy lean in towards Sammy's face, so close it looked like he was about to kiss her on the lips. We were all watching. They hugged each other.

Come on, called his mother. Let's get home for dinner.

He's a young man already, Madelaine says to me. And Sammy is changing. She's started to bud, it's the truth.

That's early, at eight, I say. But come to think of it, I hit adolescence at the same age, but I was my full height already and rounded. Sammy's so skinny.

Madelaine pours water in the kettle, arranges two mugs, the sugar bowl, carton of soy milk, and brings the tray to the table. As if she's been puzzling about it, Madelaine says, That boy may have nothing to do with anything. I don't know. I tell you these things, Mum, because I want you to know how things keep changing around here.

11

Are beef ribs good for you? James says to me in the playground. He leans a little off balance so that the zippers of his school bag face the concrete.

Yes, beef ribs are okay, I say. Protein.

I've heard James's stories – how Dad and Nana keep telling him he's fat; that he eats too much pasta. He's said his friend Andrew has an amazing six-pack, and Andrew's only nine years old. That's no six-pack, said Andrew's mother, they're his ribs sticking out. Tell Dad and Nana they should look to their own stomachs, Madelaine told him. You've got a nuggety build, like next-door-Tom, she said. You're not fat.

Come on, let's get going, James says to me now, impatience in his tone. He begins to move in the direction of the school gate.

What about Sammy? I say. She's not out of class yet.

There she is, he says. He hurries towards her, pulls her by the sleeve, and attempts to move her to the exit and my car.

She refuses to follow him. I want to ask someone over, she says to me. Please, please.

You should organise a play date beforehand, I say.

She sprints away across the schoolyard. I stand there clasping her school bag. James hollers at his sister to come back. He starts up with the counting warning: five, four, three, two…

I tell him it's okay, I'll handle it. He can wait in the car.

Where're the keys? he says. Give me the keys.

When I tell him the car is unlocked, he races off down the side of the school buildings.

Do you want to come to my place today? Sammy asks a boy playing a game of handball with a small rubber high-bouncing ball.

No, sorry, not today. The edges of the boy's school shirt flip up in the wind as he dishes up a skidding serve to his friend.

Sammy darts off to the infants' area, where she patiently plays peek-a-boo around a post with Chloe, her little school buddy.

I walk over.

The girl's mother says, That's very nice of Sammy to invite Chloe over. Chloe adores Sammy. She takes Chloe by the hand. Perhaps another day.

Come on, darling, I say to Sammy. Your brother's waiting in the car. You two can play together today.

I reach out to her. She dashes off across the concourse again.

12

In the grey dusk, which is already lengthening into summer, my daughter comes downstairs with her hair wet from the shower, dressed already in a nightie, dabbing at her damp head. She's just back from the gym. I look up at her as she descends the steps. The dinner is cooked and ready in the oven, the kids watch TV on the couch. She is clearly defined in the softening glow, and clearer again beneath the down lights over the staircase.

At the bottom of the steps, she pats her hair with the towel, front and back, and it springs into ringlets. The steam has made its way through the dusk, the essence of vanilla shampoo turning the air moist and sweet. The shine of the wooden floor increases, brown to brown, darker and darker, and on the shag pile rug the cats' fur disappears into the misted air and settles, all over the place in a grey-white film.

In the kitchen, Madelaine begins to unpack the clean dishes and cutlery. That's the thing, Mum, she says. The worst part. It's only me now who unstacks the dishwasher. Her voice takes on the contracted, disheartened tone of someone reconciled to their fate. How was Sammy for you today? she asks.

Okay. Why?

She mimics choking someone with her hands encircling their neck. She lowers her voice. My new friend, Hamish, popped in last night after dinner, she says. You wouldn't believe it. Sammy was the perfect angel. She took her empty dinner plate into the kitchen without being asked. She even put the parmesan and tomato sauce back in the fridge without me saying anything. Amazing. Madelaine moves her head from one side to the other as if watching racing cars speed by, incredulity on her face as her eyes follow the remembered sight of Sammy moving from the table to the kitchen time after time. Unheard of.

We have a laugh and shake our heads at the idea of Sammy being helpful.

She knows how to be a good girl, Madelaine says.

She must like Hamish, I say. To want to impress him.

Not necessarily. She asked me what sort of job Hamish has and if he earns a lot of money. She's probably plotting – she knows I can only afford a small place – her father in the big house with a pool that Pat went halves in. The kids are aware of how big everyone's place is.

Dreadful, I sigh. After a silence, I ask her how things are going with Hamish.

He's probably not someone for the long term, she says. That's all I can tell you. I think he's fun, Mum. You know how it is. You want to have some fun, for the sake of having a good time – because I'm not ready to be in a serious relationship. That's the thing. If he wants to spend time with me and spoil me, why not? You know. You've been through it.

13

For the sleepover at my place, my daughter has packed the kids' clothes in a canvas bag with long shoulder straps. The front of the bag is striking in design, hand-painted by Sammy – a vibrant Christmas tree in the centre. Sammy's created an imaginative piece of artwork that combines the practicality of a carry bag.

At the bottom of the satchel, Madelaine has arranged the iPod and its charger so Sammy can plug into her music at bedtime. On the top are two swimming costumes: a halter-neck one-piece and a striped red-and-white bikini. Two choices. Once, at my place, when Sammy didn't like the clothes her mother had packed for her, she sat in the suitcase and closed the lid, zipped it up and refused to come out. I had to ring Madelaine and hand the phone to Sammy through a small gap in the zip to help persuade Sammy to get out of the suitcase. We were going out for dinner. In the end, she left my house wearing only an overcoat, nothing else.

This time my daughter has also packed three cotton T-shirts, and a hand-me-down silver-spotted blouse from Sammy's cousin, May Ling, four pairs of shoes: white sandals with a slip-on big-toe section, silver sparkly canvas lace-ups, brown high-heeled wedges and white slip-ons with silver studs and a silver buckle. Next to the brightly lit Christmas tree, so we won't forget them, her rollerblades lean against the wall.

The cats greeted me when I arrived to pick the kids up, a day of scattered showers, isolated thunderstorms and light winds, the rain already pooling between the tiles in the entry foyer when I unfurled my umbrella at the door.

In the kitchen, Madelaine was preparing a bowl of hummus with carrots on the side for Sammy's breakfast. Do you want the carrot chopped up, or whole? she called out.

I don't know, Sammy said in her tired, cranky voice. She clutched at her pink-and-white fluffy dressing gown that she'd thrown over her naked body. Her toes, with the nails painted bright orange, played with her brother's feet on the couch as she lay on her stomach on the rug and hugged a pillow from the settee.

When I walked into the kitchen to say hello to my daughter, she said it was the usual daily struggle over food. Things are so much worse if Sammy hasn't eaten, she said.

Madelaine has told me Sammy rarely opens her lunch box at school, and that the food comes home untouched.

Now, when my daughter comes outside to wave us goodbye from the top of the stairs that lead to the garage, she's holding Mister Sphinx in her arms. He is lying on his back like a baby, with his paws curled in the air, purr, purr, purr. She strokes and tickles him, under the chin, down his neck, over his tummy. Tiny specks of fur float in the air as she uses the tips of her nails to give him a thorough scratch.

Sammy, now wearing her rollerblades, edges backwards down the steps.

I don't want her to break any bones when she's with me, I say to my daughter, in the hope that she'll put a stop to Sammy's progression down the stairwell.

If Sammy breaks any bones, just ring for an ambulance, my daughter retorts. She buries her lips into Mister Sphinx's furry head. Just ring for an ambulance, she repeats. And then you'll be rid of her.

Her tone is matter-of-fact, the words spoken as if they could speak for themselves, as if things in the town house – James, the cats, the woollen rug, the Christmas tree with its lights, the long wooden dining table – would collectively concur with this statement.

From where James and I wait at the bottom of the stairs holding the bag and Sammy's scooter, I glower up at my daughter.

She kisses the cat's head. See, she says nodding towards Sammy. Sammy can rollerblade backwards down a flight of stairs.

14

When Sammy stayed at my place, I'd open up one of my books on Egypt where I knew she'd look at the pictures and I'd tell her some of the myths. We'd lie on the bed at night time. Look, I'd say, a story about a crocodile. There's a picture of the sacred crocodile. The Egyptian priests have tamed him and fed him cakes and honey wine. And here's Sobek, the crocodile god. See Sobek, the man with a crocodile's head on the River Nile? The waves, rolling over themselves, fanning out sideways from the headland, leave behind the woolly sea. He's watching the shore, all the way across. A breath of wind ruffles the waters of the lake shaded by acacias, swaying date palms and fig trees laden with fruit. Look, ducks, geese, and fish swimming among lotus petals. Sobek notices sand dunes drifting against granite but his vision is blurred, and the hieroglyphics are unintelligible. He turns over the tablet – we can see the squiggly letters – maybe they're upside down, or backwards – and on the other side, where we cannot see, is recorded a song about an Egyptian family on an outing. See the daughter, she's picking lotus blossoms from the papyrus raft. Even the family cats have come on the picnic with them. And here's a painting of a girl carrying lotuses and ducks gathered during a hunting trip with her father. Her nickname is Miw, a word that means 'little cat'.

Do you want to hear the story of the cat-goddess, Sammy? Do you want me to read to you, or don't you?

And then I might sing her the song of an Egyptian mother called Nefertiti. There she is, I'll say. Her name means 'the beautiful woman has come'. Here she is with one of her daughters.

It's a happy happy song that a scribe has written down on the tablet.

She looks like the soaring star at dawn,

At the beginning of new year,
Brilliant glow, pale of skin,
Pretty the look of her eyes,
Kind the words from her lips…
With nimble step she strides the earth,
Enchants my spirit by her actions,
She causes all men's heads
To spin around to gaze at her;
Delight has he whom she enfolds,
He is like a man reborn.

15

Boundaries, consequences. That's what they tell you, my daughter said. Setting boundaries, being consistent. Praise rather than reprimand. To teach her to behave appropriately through the consistent and exhaustive reinforcement of good behaviour over a sustained period. It works, I'm told. My daughter grabbed the words from the air, her eyes turned to the side and then up at the wall. It's not easy, she sighed.

Sammy was born like this, I reassured her. It's not your fault.

16

May Ling, my eldest grandchild, with her wide white face and her jet-black straight hair pulled back under a fedora hat, could easily pass for a fifteen-year-old when she comes over to my place with her younger brother, Alexander, for a play with Sammy and James. But she wears loose denim shorts and a large dark blue T-shirt that disguise her changing twelve-year-old body.

Playing handball, Alexander throws with the strength of a cricket fast bowler, the ball bouncing off the wall with great force. His hair is the same black as his sister's, and devoid of curl or kink, so fine and straight it flops and floats when he jumps for a catch, like hair caught in mid-flight by a slow-motion camera. But his eyebrows are a thick solid black against his white skin.

Sammy loves that fedora hat. She admires its beauty; she envies May Ling and tells her, I want your hat. I want a hat just like that.

Because of the black fedora, May Ling is extra tall and Sammy can't swipe it off her head. But when May Ling and Sammy come downstairs from the bedroom, Sammy is wearing the hat.

The two of them sit at the kitchen table eating orange quarters I've cut up for morning tea. Alexander and James are playing table tennis in the attic. They'll take a break at the end of the game. The two girls bite into the flesh of the oranges, and look around the kitchen at me. I am the housekeeper. What would they do without me, with my plates of food, catering to all tastes, anticipating their needs? Out the window, the sun on a spider's web strung up between the wisteria and frangipani branches, transforms it into a golden mandala. Another weaving clings to the corner of the ceiling in the kitchen.

When it's time to go home and my son arrives to pick up May Ling and Alexander, I call upstairs, Dad's here. Time to go home.

Can't they stay? Sammy calls back down. I want them to stay and have a sleepover with us, she says.

Maybe next time, May Ling and Alexander's father says. Maybe in the school holidays.

With the fedora back on her head, May Ling slips her feet into jewelled thongs and nods. I'll need to bring pyjamas and a toothbrush, she says. She slides the hat off her head and her hair puffs out a little at the sides, a lank, thick straightness. She shakes her head like a person nodding 'yes', then 'no', and the hair spins away from her shoulders and puffs out some more. See you in the holidays, then! she says.

17

Sammy's defiant nature, her refusal to be cooperative, the power of her opposition, her determination to haul her wiry frame arm to arm across the monkey bars, her hand-made mosaics in the shape of butterflies and pussy cats, her need for recognition. She is the sleeping beauty. But how do you awaken her to a world of conformity?

<h1 style="text-align:center">18</h1>

Sammy scoots along the footpath towards the shops, her scooter a pink and silver rider with a foot brake at the back. The mould is metal, designed and produced in China, so the vehicle on wheels, unhinged and secured at its joints to its framework, presents a steely exterior to the world. It is collapsible and able to disintegrate into small pieces like the wings of a butterfly.

At the top of the hill, the narrow walkway is congested – dogs on leads, elderly people with walking sticks, children. James and I follow behind Sammy, me calling to watch out as her leg swings back and forth scootering high in the air. She is just ahead of us, her left leg moving back and forth as a man with a stick comes towards us; he stops and steps to the side of the path.

At the doorway of the newsagent, James is ready to order a newspaper for me and to check out the special connector textas he says he needs to buy in order to do some drawings at my place. Sammy shifts impatiently back and forth on her scooter wanting, in a pleading voice, to look at the purple box of lollies two rows beneath the cash register. I stand there firm by the doorway, in spite of her begging, and wait for James to appear, for him to hand me my newspaper – if only I can keep Sammy out of the shop. That's how it always is.

Back at my place, preparing the evening meal, all is quiet. Sammy sits on the couch holding the TV remote, leaning back on the cushions. James is at the table drawing on white paper. I ask Sammy to turn the television off, tell her dinner is ready.

She ignores me.

You know, in my house people don't watch TV while eating, I say. I make a grab for the remote and press the red button.

Sammy gets up from the settee, stamps into the bedroom and slams the door.

Is she like this at Dad's? I ask James.

Yes. But she's worst for Nana. It's an anger management problem, he says.

Someone else in your family has that issue, I murmur half to myself.

His eyebrows knit together in thought as he joins up the connector pens at their lids. Who? he says. He's been drawing a Christmas tree and filled the page with colour, but now he's crumpling the paper up.

Can I see what you drew? I ask.

No, he says, I've made a mistake. Where's the bin?

Sammy is silent in the bedroom; probably listening to James and me on the other side of the door, locked in there, defiantly, as a statement, so that she is set apart from us. I wait.

When she slides her hand under the door, I notice it, put my palm on top of hers and tell her I hate fighting like this. Let's kiss and make up, I say through the door.

Kisses, well, she still struggles with kisses. I knock gently. She makes an animal-like squeak. I open the door an inch or two and then enter the room. She is lying on a pillow on the floor. Her eyes, a leopard's golden hue, just like her father's, glimmer in the darkened room. I creep in and we hug each other and then she comes out. You learn to either approach slowly and carefully, or you walk straight in. Each time it's slightly easier.

In the morning, when their mother comes to pick them up, I tell her all went well except for the one incident with the TV.

I'm glad you did it, Mum, she says. Sammy needs to know.

I look at Sammy standing at the front door, ready to take the overnight bag to the car. She's grown so tall, almost to my shoulders already. In the space between us, my daughter tells the children to say thanks for having me. Then they jump down the stairs and disappear around the stairwell.

19

My daughter said, When Mister Sphinx hadn't been home for four nights I desperately searched the streets and the downstairs garages. The kids were at their dad's. When Sammy got back and I told her the news, she was frantic. She wanted to know when I'd last seen the cat. When I was walking to the bus stop to go to work, I told her. He followed me to the end of the street. I waved him goodbye. Sammy said we needed to leave immediately to begin a search. Hurry, she said. We need to get going. So we checked the loft above the pull-down ladder again. And then down to the garages to have another look. After that we came back in and I made up some Lost Cat posters with a photo and phone number to stick to the telegraph poles. Turns out a man down the road had taken Mister Sphinx in, fed him bowls of milk, and very much wanted to keep him for himself. But he saw the posters and rang the number. Aren't we lucky?

Yes, I said. Disaster averted.

I could hear the pride in Sammy's voice when I picked the children up from school the next day and she told me that she and Mummy had made a poster with Mister Sphinx's photo on it. She wound the window down as she spoke, catching the breeze, breathing in the fresh air, gulping it down.

The wind through the car window snared her feral hair, long and knotted now that the tiny beaded plaits had grown out, and we could feel the calming breeze in the air, separating the matted strands and untangling it. She pointed to the telegraph posts as we drove past, showing where they'd stuck the posters.

Where did you get the pictures of Mister Sphinx? I asked.

Mum got them off the computer, she said. She shook the hair away from her eyes.

Let's try some plaits when we get home, I said.

She screwed up her face at me. No, she shouted.

It's okay, darling, I said. It's okay. I was only making a suggestion.

Back at the town house, Sammy and James hopped out of the car and ran up the stairs to their front door. I took the bags of food for dinner out of the boot.

Sammy called out to me, Hurry up and unlock the door.

20

Sitting here at my desk, I'm thinking about how hard it is to understand Sammy, in all of her wildness and complexity.

I am looking at two photographs of Sammy, both in school uniform. One is at seven and the other is at eight. When she is seven, she smiles for the photographer and shows the gaps in her teeth. In the second photo, there are no gaps and the smile is more forced. Her funny little lopsided smile.

After the first day of the new school term, she said she wasn't going back to school. Tell them I've been hit by a bus, she said to her mother. And I'm dead.

Poor Sammy. Poor Madelaine. Poor James. Poor me. On and on it goes.

Four weeks into the school term and things continued to get worse and worse. Sammy was put into the Naughty Kids group. All boys, except Sammy. The good kids were in a group with a smiley face on top. The naughty kids sat beneath an unhappy face. She'd been in the Naughty Kids group since the first day, when she didn't get her writing done in time and was forbidden to go outside to play.

I heard Madelaine's accounts of the screaming sessions in the mornings, when she struggled to get Sammy ready for school, and her refusal to do homework. She'd shown Sammy the times table at the back of the homework book and how to make a line across with a ruler to find the answers. The more I try to explain, the more agitated she becomes, Madelaine said. Sammy says it's too hard, and that if I let her have some playtime now, she'll do the homework in the morning. At least when she went next door to play with Vincent and his baby sister, I was free to help James with his homework. Later, when I went to get her, Vincent's mother said she'd been a fabulous help and had given the baby her dinner.

One of my daughter's doctor friends suggested Sammy be seen by a psychiatrist. The friend said she wouldn't forgive herself if she didn't speak up, she continued. That things can be done when children are still young. She said it would be awful to find out when Sammy is seventeen that something could have been done to help her. But Sammy's father and Nana refused to let her go. They said they didn't want her taken out of school for another appointment.

The thing is, I'm worried about Sammy being labelled, my daughter said. Anyway, it's not as if she's likely to have ADHD – you know how engrossed she gets when she's doing her craft. And I don't want her taking medication. It's not as if we got anywhere with that last psychologist. After all those visits, and all that money, all he could say was, he'd never, in his thirty-five years of being a child specialist, seen a kid so determined. We left there with a box full of behaviour management tools, but so far nothing has changed. Now we've got a referral to a paediatrician.

James told me he's fed up with his sister. At eleven, he'd transformed into an angry, surly boy. His mother said it's the hormones already causing mood swings, but James has complained repeatedly that he gets no let-up from his sister. You and Dad get a break every seven days, Mum, but I get no break at all, he said. He suggested to his mother that she should send Sammy to boarding school.

It's okay, Madelaine reassured him. You don't have to find a solution to the problem.

Another humid summer's day. I've decided to walk to the lily pond in Centennial Park. I'm carrying my book of Egyptian myths. I stop at a café by the side of the road, where there's a cool breeze. Music wafts out on to the street. People walk past in their hats and dark sunglasses. One woman uses a tangerine umbrella to shade her from the sun. The hum of voices behind me. It's hard to think. There's always someone talking too loudly at these places. One person who talks, and the other who is silent. I lick the chocolate cloud off the rim of the cup. The coffee is thick and hot and eases the aching in my throat.

My mobile disturbs the moment. As I put it away again, I can still hear my daughter's voice, and the odd splashing sound as she adjusted her position in the bath. If the paediatrician decides Sammy needs medication, she said, it will give everyone a break. I knew better than to comment.

I open my book and read the story of the lotus blossom that appeared out of the dark and dismal expanse of flood waters that had engulfed the world at the mythical beginning of time. The blossom surfaced and opened its petals to give birth to the sun. I hold on to this Egyptian symbol of something beautiful breaking through from the darkness.

Part Two

1

There are so many ways that it is possible to make a mistake, I am coming to understand – various, unexpected ways; when unaware, out of the blue, a hidden obstacle, and an accident happens. There are the responsible and the irresponsible ways. I said so myself. We all make mistakes. Accidents happen. We run an amber light or cross a road, not carefully enough.

Madelaine's father rings from the snowfields. Madelaine's had an accident, he says.

I imagine my daughter's white ski jacket splattered with blood. It sounds at first like the other time he'd rung. Don't worry, he'd said. She'll be okay. Her ear lobe had been sliced by a ski.

This time, he says, she landed on her head. A ski jump. She's been hallucinating.

Where is she now? I ask.

In the hospital. She's in Cooma hospital. The doctors said it's lucky she was wearing a helmet. The helmet was smashed to bits. They'll tell us more after the tests. She'll be okay.

I want to tell him, What are you talking about, she'll be okay? In her bruised brain, her mind would be telling her that she did something stupid. She didn't check the size of the jump. No warning signs. Just the words, Enter at your own risk. A man-made series of jumps. She'll make it to the other side; she'll hold on and accelerate just when we start to worry, she'll open her eyes, lift her head, get up. She goes limp in the snow; she gives herself up to the ski patrol; she doesn't make it across to the other side.

She's in the best place, he says. We're all here with her.

All right, I say. And I say to myself, I can see my daughter. It is a simple mantra, and I do see her, in the mornings, just out of bed. I see her from the front door, from the side. She's wearing those pink pyjamas with the animal print and the television is on. She stretches her legs out along the couch, comfortably, on the black leather lounge, leaning back on the arm rest, the remote in her hand.

She'll be okay, her father repeats.

I'm okay, my daughter could say. Or not. She could say those simple words, I'm not okay. Why didn't she say them when trapped by a jealous and controlling man – held captive in an invisible cage?

2

A week after the accident, when they all returned from the snow, my daughter sent me a text: Back home safe. Can you come over tomorrow?

In the garage beneath the town house I lift the bags of food out of the boot and walk up the stairs to their front door. I knock and let myself in.

Sammy walks towards me, pulling the pink and white dressing gown closed across her bare body, using the tie at the waist to secure it. The closer Sammy gets, the more in focus she becomes – suntanned face, white goggle marks around her eyes; her face divided in sections by the lines between one part and the other. Mummy's waiting for you to make breakfast, she says. She can't use her hands.

Oh, I say. I didn't know her hands were injured.

She won't have a shower till you get here, Sammy says. She's still dizzy.

That's no good, sweetheart. I thought she was a lot better.

She didn't want me to sleep in her bed last night, says Sammy, but I did. I wanted to sleep next to her like I usually do. But Mummy told me I'm selfish. She's sleeping all the time. She asked if we know about ringing triple zero if she goes unconscious. I said I know. And I'll ask James to give them our address.

James plays computer games at the desk between the lounge room and the kitchen. We're meant to be at Dad's this week, he calls out, but Dad hasn't picked us up yet. Poor Mum, he says. She didn't have much of a holiday. Poor Mum. You should have seen Samantha's face when they told her Mum had an accident and has concussion.

As I walk up the stairs to Madelaine's room, I wonder if Sammy knows what the word concussion means.

My daughter is asleep, the white doona loosely draped across her feet, and one arm, still showing the bruise from a cannula, rests on the blanket.

Both her thumbs are encased in black splints. Her head is turned slightly to the right on the pillow, hiding the bandage across her nose, her face red, her hair damp with perspiration. I walk over to the bed and put my hand gently on her forehead. Does she have a temperature? No, not hot. I sit down on the side of the bed. I can hear the television downstairs, and I hear the sound of my daughter breathing, in and out through the mouth. I look at her face, sit there, watching over her. I didn't know she'd be like this. It's me, I say. I'm here.

She makes a sighing sound.

Do you think you should spend so much time sleeping? I ask her.

I'm resting my brain, she whispers. It's good.

Sixteen hours a day? That's what you said to the doctor. Didn't he say you've rested your brain enough?

Her eyes stay closed, but her mouth with the lips slightly apart, begins a new sound with every breath.

Why don't you sit up and I'll bring you a cup of tea? I say.

She opens her eyes, tries to lift herself from the pillow and to rest her back against the bedhead. It's a struggle, but she does it.

I bring the tea upstairs and a bowl of breakfast cereal. She's lying down again with her eyes closed.

Wake up, darling, I say. Have a cup of tea. It might make you feel better.

She grunts and stays where she is. I know that crying is no help to her, so I leave the room to compose myself. It may be a stroke, the neurologist had said. Worst case scenario, a stroke.

Worst case scenario. Madelaine would have blocked those words out. Words she would never take to. It can't be. Things will be the same as before. I know it. Things will return to how they were before.

I go back in to her room and whisper, I'm worried about you, darling. I didn't know things were this bad. I'm not sure what to do.

Ring the neurologist, she slurs the words. He'll tell you what to do.

I make the phone call, tell the doctor she seems to be getting worse.

Take her straight to Emergency, he says. I'll meet you there.

I pull my daughter up into a sitting position and swing her legs over the side of the bed, so I can push slippers on to her feet. In the cupboard I find a black wool overcoat she can wear over her pyjamas. We all get in my car and I drive to the hospital.

3

The four of us were settled on chairs outside the doors to the emergency ward: Madelaine, Sammy, James and me. The neurologist had said hospital was the best place, in case anything further needed to be done. As we waited, Sammy played peek-a-boo with a child in a stroller using the big brown envelope that contained the X-rays. The child had eaten a spider. His face was red and swollen. When Madelaine made it to the head of the queue, she told the child's mother they could go first.

I reached for the envelope. Thanks Sammy, I said. We'll give it to the doctor when he gets here. He's just across the road, so he should be here soon.

Sammy paid close attention to the injured and the disabled, lined up on chairs behind us. I'd seen her before, watching the way a blind person would tap his way along a footpath, or a person with a withered limb enter a swimming pool, then she'd practise the funny movements that she'd observed. She was alert to all difference. Compassionate. Given any collection of people, Sammy believed there were things to watch out for; it was a pastime, a hobby, like learning to sing. She would absorb what was happening around her with her own eyes. You learn about life that way.

When Madelaine was shown in through the doors by a uniformed nurse wearing sensible shoes, I asked if we could all come too. That's fine, she said. You can stay with her. Just keep the children quiet and on a chair.

Come on, Sammy and James, I said. Follow me. We'll go in.

Yellow exit tape showed us the way along the corridor. The nurse's shoes squeaked across the rubbery floor. When she handed Madelaine a white hospital gown to change into, I asked if I could give Madelaine the toasted sandwich I'd bought at the hospital shop. She hasn't had anything to eat yet, I said. She gets low blood sugar and gets faint if she doesn't eat.

No, the nurse said in a clipped tone. No food and nothing to drink. She pulled a curtain around the bed and squeakily departed.

An examining doctor, a young Irish woman with long blonde hair tied in a plait down her back, dressed in what looked like a green cotton tracksuit, introduced herself and then disappeared behind the curtain to do the tests: head, neck, eye movements. She'd seen the X-rays and told us the MRI was the most important. A muffled buzz caused her to walk away quickly to another screened-off area where lights were flashing and nurses rushing in. Later, we learnt someone had gone into cardiac arrest.

When another nurse opened up the curtain we saw that Madelaine's sprained hands, with their torn ligaments and damaged nerves, had been bandaged up to her elbows. She lay back pale, clasping the iron bars along the side of the bed, as if afraid she'd fall out. The testing had made her dizzy.

I put the black coat on a chair on one side of the bed, and Sammy and James shared a seat on the other.

Sammy noticed her mother's wrapped-up hands and came over to the bed to examine them. She moved each bruised thumb around gently in its socket, one at a time, like an examining doctor. Which one is the hurtiest? she asked her mother.

Madelaine shook her head and smiled at her daughter.

I sat in a chair next to the bed, and that's where I was still when the neurologist arrived. His name was Dr Kreymer. I don't like to ring Dr Kreymer too early, the Irish doctor had said. Dr Kreymer introduced himself. A broad-shouldered man, not tall or heavy but burly; one had an impression of solidness. His manner was kind and reassuring. He wore a midnight-blue striped suit with a white shirt and grey tie, and black and white shiny shoes that Sammy noticed immediately. His hair was a mass of unruly curls, left to fall across his forehead and over his ears. Dr Kreymer riffled through the documents in the envelope. He'd seen the X-rays. He checked Madelaine's neck, while using a machine that enabled him to see her eyes in close up as he moved her head gently from side to side.

Sammy was sitting very straight on the metal chair, being the perfect child, with one knee crossed on the other and her linked hands resting on her thigh.

Dr Kreymer asked questions of Madelaine as if playing for time: What day of the week is it? How did the accident happen? Did you lose consciousness? What work do you do? How old are the children? How many hours a day are you sleeping? Sixteen still?

At last he was finished with the questioning and spoke, giving the impression that he had been able to understand Madelaine. There was nothing studied about his assuredness, nothing theatrical. Madelaine hoisted herself up to a sitting position.

Dr Kreymer looked at her in calm, mild-mannered confidence, his eyebrows almost a straight thick black line. Bad concussion and whiplash, he said showing perfect white teeth in a knowing smile. But you have a beautiful brain, Madelaine. Look at this X-ray.

When he clipped the X-rays up, we all studied the brain mass pictures as he tapped the monitor. Sammy's hands were in her lap. She looked at the shapes on the screen, frowning, as if she didn't know what to make of it all.

A very beautiful brain, Dr Kreymer repeated. And it's large. There's nothing wrong with it.

Thank you, Madelaine said politely in a voice that seemed to come from a long way off. Yes, more distantly still, thank you. She nodded to herself.

Dr Kreymer, as if satisfied, gave her a friendly smile and said she should start using her brain again. You've rested it long enough, he said. And you can start a little gentle exercise each day. I'm going to write you a letter to a physio for the whiplash.

Sammy, on the other side of the bed, swung her legs, her hands secured beneath them on the seat.

Dr Kreymer turned to her. I've got a daughter your age, he said. She's eight going on thirty. Much more grown-up than her older brother.

We all looked at James, cross-legged, slumped forward over one knee, chin in hand, his right thumb working at his iPod touch.

My son is a very grown-up young man, Madelaine said softly, with a sad, resigned tone.

Next to him on the chair, Sammy shifted her legs, making the metal creak. Through the summer, her hair had turned from rich brown to light brown, almost as fair as her mother's, and from where I sat on the other side of the bed that morning, her face merged with that of her mother's. If I glanced at Sammy, what I saw was a young woman with long straight hair, streaked with blonde, a young woman with her eyes wide open, examining the apparatus around the bed. She might have had a third eye, if I'd concentrated hard enough to imagine it.

Part Three

1

The message on Sammy's cake was Happy Birthday, with a blue icing number 9 underneath. May Ling carried the cake into the room with candles aglow. As we sang, Sammy, at the end of the table, lifted her arms in time like a conductor. When we were finished, she grinned her big smile, and I saw every one of her perfect white teeth.

Later, she scrolled down the birthday photos on her mother's phone. Look, she said to me. See the cake? A castle. There are the flags and the decorations and there is the door. Mummy and me made it using Smarties and fizzy things and those liquorice lollies and musk sticks. See, my brother's still wearing his football clothes. He had that red thing in his mouth that he puts in when he plays footy, so his lips look funny as they open and close.

And you're wearing May Ling's black hat, I said. Would you like me to buy you a hat like that for your birthday?

No thanks, she said. I like a surprise. She scrolled down the phone some more. And this is a photo of me and a girl that I drew, she laughed. The drawing is almost as big as me. See, I used real material for the dress.

2

Whenever May Ling came through the front door and walked towards Sammy to say hello, Sammy automatically reached up and pulled at May Ling's fedora hat, clamped tightly to her head. As Sammy reached up for the hat, May Ling would tickle her cousin under the arms and then chase her around the house, but always with laughter, like a fun-loving big sister. She'd put up a struggle and then hand over a decorated envelope which Sammy ripped open with her fingernails – a beautiful card she'd make each year for Sammy's birthday – usually an elaborate castle drawing or a fantasy palace or a temple, maybe a troll with candy-corn coloured horns, or an Egyptian god: half-woman, half-cat.

I told May Ling one afternoon, Your drawings are exquisite. I'm going to frame that one of the girl's face with blonde hair and Asian eyes. A plain white frame to match its simplicity.

No way, she said. I don't want you to. It's not good enough to put in a frame. I want to take it back.

It's okay, darling, I said. I heard you. I won't frame it if you don't want me to.

We were walking together up and down the aisles at a drapery store, making our way in between all the big rolls of fabric. Alexander trailed behind, bouncing his rubber ball.

May Ling was looking for material to make an outfit for a dress-up role-play party set in Cleopatra's palace. A group of characters would be adventuring together in a role-playing game. She was looking for something lime-green to use with the black cotton she'd bought already.

You're spoiling her, Alexander said as his sister walked on ahead.

See if you can find something you'd like me to buy you, I said as we looked for his ball, now lost under the tables of textiles.

You shouldn't keep buying May Ling things, he said. You're spending too much money.

Let's have a look here in this fancy dress section. What about a sparkly tap dancer's hat and cane, or a magician's outfit for you?

No thanks, he said. Wow. Look at these bubble-making guns.

You can choose one of those and blow bubbles over my balcony.

He looked at me. I don't know which one to get. What do you think?

You decide, darling. Which one do you like best?

You could buy a ready-made outfit from here, I called out to May Ling. Lots of fancy dress costumes here.

I don't like buying clothes, she said. I like to make my own outfits. But Sammy does. You should bring Sammy here.

That's a thought, I said. I will. In the school holidays.

And that's when I knew what I could get for Sammy. You hear yourself think something and then you hear yourself say what it is you need to do.

I didn't have long to wait. The next Saturday, I picked Sammy up and took her on a buying expedition to the same shopping centre. In a bargain department store on the top level, we bought five new outfits and two pairs of canvas lace-up shoes. The whole process was so quick and easy I couldn't believe we were having such a non-combative time together. Our only disagreement was about the sizing. Sammy wanted small and tight and I wanted room for growth.

When we walked outside the store, she turned her head to the left and to the right and said she wanted to look in some more shops.

More shops? I said. I've spent a lot of money already, darling.

She leaned her head forward and sucked in a mouthful of air, then parted her lips and, with great force, sighed, I know. I've got an idea, she said. I've got some money in my piggy bank. A fifty-dollar note. You use your money now and I'll pay you back when we get home. Okay?

All right. I guess so.

I felt her hand relax in my hand as I led the way to the escalator. She wanted to find a shop she'd seen on the way up. We rode the escalator down to the basement, then up, then down again. But she couldn't find it.

She screwed up her face in frustration, saying, I saw it before.

What do you want to buy?

I'll see.

What kind of shop?

I'll find it, she said, letting go of the handrail and jumping off the moving stairs and running down an arcade.

I ran after her.

She pointed to clouds painted across a glass window. There it is.

Oh. Here? A sleepwear shop?

Yes! Her face was flushed with the explosive ejection of the word.

There are children's pyjamas down the back, I said. And some kids' stationery.

Yes! Yes, I can see them.

Knowing it would be a very long process for Sammy to decide what she wanted to buy, I sat down on the concrete floor, my back against the wall, and waited. I watched while she looked around the shop with an enthusiasm I hadn't seen in months, first the pyjamas, then the stationery. When she'd inspected thoroughly every item in the store, she took a matching cat-motifed wallet and iPod cover to the counter after first checking with me that they didn't cost more than $50.

On the way back home, she reached down to the car radio, changed the station to Nova 969, and bobbed her head to the beat. When we reached the house, I followed her into the lounge room, where she extracted the crumpled-up note out of the bottom of her piggy bank. I gave her a $20 note in change. She pulled the clothes and shoes out of the bags and spread them out on the floor to show Mummy and James when they came home.

Her eyes were hypnotised now by the television, and she stretched out on her stomach, her chin in her hands. Mister Sphinx purred rhythmically from his curled-up position on her spine. It was easy for me to see her more clearly today. I didn't want to imagine, in the spaces behind her eyes, the uncontrollable emotions, hovering there, of any number of oppositional behaviours. There should be spaces for negotiation, room for control of her defiance. Things could be worse. Much worse. Autism, Asperger's. Somewhere, out of sight, everything was in a state of flux.

3

How many ways it would have been possible to be more supportive to Sammy, I was coming to understand – the food additives and sugars, the controllable, understandable ways, the strict, the consistent, predictable, sensible and not-sensible ways. Use lots of praise, said Sammy's teacher. Praise, praise, praise.

I imagined harmony. I saw Sammy jumping on the trampoline out the back, smiling her funny lopsided grin, happy like any other nine-year-old child.

Madelaine said things were good that week. It sounded at first as if there'd been a shift in the weather.

4

Harmony Day, all of it, all of it was already far behind. Out through the windscreen of the car, leaving the school playground, was the sound of rain. I saw the splattering on the glass, and with the wet, came the breeze through the window, the autumn light on the leaves, the thick gnarled trunk of the magnolia tree. I wound up the windows of the car. The blue sky disappeared, up beyond the clouds.

I strapped the seat belt across me with a snap, but the glimpses of grey afternoon between the tree branches, the weather outside, had already begun to diminish. Everything became silent and faded in colour – the whole Harmony Day, all of it, all of the songs and the holding hands in a circle and the wearing of orange clothing, the teachers' instructions, the dancing around the rose garden, the flowers in heady bloom – it was all left behind.

I drove away, across the bitumen, down through the slope of the hill. When I turned on the demister, the cleared area of the glass expanded, and lifted. The opening of an eye. This was not new, this clarity; this was the same antagonism every ex-wife and ex-mother-in-law can be forced to face at these school events.

The windows cleared front and back, and I turned the radio off, not wanting its distraction.

The children had been sitting at their desks, first to sixth grade, for the arrival of the grandparents. Fourth grade, Sammy's grade, were cutting and pasting, readers on the ready beside them on the desk. Boys and girls, wearing something tangerine or red and yellow.

The invitation said, The children have been busy preparing for Harmony Day and Grandparents Day.

I'd seen the other grandmother standing talking to her husband in the car park, a cigarette hanging out the corner of her mouth as she spoke, her umbrella in one hand, handbag on her shoulder, a flowing floral skirt, long white cotton top, her hair secured tightly at the back with a clip.

No finger pointing, my ex-husband had said through the long cold lens of the telephone line. Finger pointing doesn't help anyone, he'd said. Anyway, she's just as critical about you.

All morning, I'd kept my jaw tight in my skull. In the car, I relaxed the muscles of my face, as much as I could and inhaled deeply, but my jaw still ached. Outside the window, the sky closed in and pressed lower. It is impossible to know how many grandparents there have been, powerless, everywhere, under overcast skies, or others even – lofty, glare-filled skies, smooth unblemished skies – all saying nothing.

I am clear about my role. I am Mummy Two, not Mummy One and, in point of fact, I have no say at all.

What is Harmony Day? I asked James.

You know, he said. The Aborigines and all that.

5

When I arrived at the school at the end of the day, Sammy saw me through her classroom window. She hurried down the steps with her friend Lewis. We followed him in search of his father to ask if the boy could come over for a play.

Back at the town house, when Lewis and Sammy were upstairs playing hidings and my daughter had returned from the gym, I said to Madelaine that Lewis's dad seemed like a nice man.

His ex-wife is a friend of mine, she said witheringly. I'd never do that. Go out with a friend's ex-husband. Anyway, he's a control freak too, and always putting her down.

I looked across the kitchen bench to Madelaine in her black lycra tights and top as she flicked through the mail on the table, her gym bag still on her shoulder. With her hair still damp and pulled back, brushed up and off the back of her neck, I could see the dark smudge of her neck tats. I wanted to say to her, What about Pat? What about your old friend Pat moving in with your ex-husband?

Instead, I said, Well, Lewis's dad appeared nice. He seemed a friendly fellow.

She said, The same with Brad. You just don't know. Who would know what Brad is really like? You have to live with someone to find out.

I try not to think of those years when Brad kept Madelaine away from us – how he isolated her from her friends and family. The accumulation, over the years, of small things, until she came to look more and more like someone who'd had the light taken out of her eyes. Was it shame? My daughter. A loving, caring, beautiful woman, who fought to get out. He's reeled me back in again, she'd tell me by text message. Her forgiving nature, always trying to see the good, even in him, the man who defined her by the post-natal depression.

When Lewis's dad arrived, I looked at him leaning against the door frame. A tall man, someone who his children had come to rely on.

He reached for his son's hand. We're just having sausages for dinner tonight, he said to his son. Where are your shoes, mate? Where did you leave them?

Lewis's dad walked towards me, in wrinkled work trousers and a business shirt with its collar open at the neck. The closer he got, the more detailed he was – light brown eyebrows, blond hair cropped above his ears, expressive mouth; there were distinct separations in each section of his face.

Say thanks for having me to Sammy's grandma, he said.

I picked up Lewis's school hat from the pile of clothes beside the front door and pointed to the black school shoes lying on the carpet. When Lewis picked them up, sand spilled out on to the rug.

Madelaine, still wearing her gym gear, and her body, outlined in lycra, glistening still with sweat, descended the steps. Her face wore a welcoming smile as she approached the door. Say goodbye to Lewis, she called back up to Sammy, who was still in her favourite hiding place.

Goodbye, Sammy called out in a muffled voice.

Madelaine walked out to the front gate with Lewis and his dad. In the courtyard, I heard them talk about the friendship between the two children. How he'd forgotten that Lewis came to Sammy's swim party, and that he thought Sammy was a new friend.

You just can't tell, Madelaine said when she came back inside. He does seem nice, she said. His wife is dating one of the other school dads. But the dad has his kids on different weekends to her, so the two of them never have a break.

6

In the kitchen, Madelaine is supervising James's homework.

Sammy has agreed that I can run a bath for her. She steps out of her clothes in the upstairs bathroom. She stands in the water, a collection of little plastic characters float on the surface, the water up to her knees, and she reaches for the box behind the bath to select some more. Her hair hangs loose; I should find a shower cap. But I stay sitting on the closed seat of the toilet, beside the bath and I watch her. What else can I do? Downstairs, I hear my daughter and grandson at the dining room table talking about homework. I can't hear their words. But I hear the splash of water as another creature is thrown against the glass shower screen and bounces into the water.

I look at myself in the mirror, bring my hand up slowly to my hair. If Sammy turned round, she would see me. I take off the orange scarf tied around my hair. My Harmony Day scarf. It all goes away – the whole day.

I watch Sammy. Look at that, I laugh. Watching. Plop, another creature lands in the water.

Mummy, she calls out. I need you. Come here.

I'm here, I say. Mummy Two is here. What do you want?

I want Mummy One.

Mummy is helping James with his homework, I say. I'm here. I keep on watching. I'm right here.

7

Madelaine

Who would have thought? It just didn't occur to me. What happened was, I lost my wallet. I was rushing off to the gym and couldn't find it anywhere. Before I left the house, I said to the kids, have either of you seen my wallet? It was the last day of the school holidays and Mum had come over in the afternoon to help with the kids. She'd mentioned that she'd seen James pull the charger for his iPod out of my handbag. My bag was lying open on the floor at the bottom of the stairs.

Mum asked James if he could remember seeing my wallet in my handbag when he pulled the charger out.

'You don't take something out of someone's bag and then look around to see what else is in there,' he said to Mum in his new rude voice.

'I wasn't accusing you of anything,' Mum had said to him. 'I just thought you might have noticed what else was in the bag. We're trying to work out when Mummy's wallet was last seen.'

That's when I remembered that I'd noticed a packet of crisps in Sammy's room that she must have taken out of my bag. 'So, Sammy,' I said, 'when you took those packets of crisps out of my bag, did you notice if my wallet was still in there?'

Sammy shook her head.

I tried to remember when I'd last seen my purse. I'd kept my bag on my lap on the bus on the way home from work with the kids. I remembered that.

'Well, then the wallet must have fallen out of your bag between the bus stop and walking to the car,' said James.

I'd checked the car and even driven past the bus stop in the dark, but I couldn't see anything. I was frantic. All my cash, my credit cards, photos of the kids, prepaid vouchers, and so on. Automatic payments to be cancelled. My whole being plummeted. I felt I'd been coping up to that moment, but then I felt myself collapse into a heap.

I'd taken the kids into work that morning. So we got back here at about three. Sammy was overtired and hadn't eaten much. Always a toxic mix. She was exhausted from the week at her dad's, tired from a late night the night before when we had dinner with my friend Graeme. So when we got back from the city in the afternoon, she started up with the whining. 'I'm bored. I've got nothing to do.' James had a friend over to play but Sammy hadn't been able to organise a play date. So I suggested all sorts of things that she could do, some craft work, a game with grandma, but each time I spoke she got angrier and angrier, until she was screaming at me.

'Why don't you just walk away from her?' Mum had suggested tentatively. She knows I'm not much for listening to her ideas about things around here. I told her that Sammy would just follow me if I moved away. But after matching up the socks in the laundry basket, I went upstairs to have a rest and to check my telephone before heading out to the gym. Mum stayed downstairs with Sammy. The boys were playing upstairs in James's room.

It was when I was packing my bag for the gym that I noticed that my purse was missing from my handbag. I panicked big time. As I said, cash, credit cards. I had no way of accessing any money. That's one of the things with having no partner. You've got no one to ask, 'Can I get some money out of your account?' Mum gave me fifty dollars to buy some milk and bread on the way to the gym, but that was it. I was stuffed. And that's when I crashed. How could I have lost my wallet? Couldn't I get anything right? What's going to go wrong next?

After the training session and the search near the bus stop in the dark, Mum had dinner on the table. I'd whispered to her in the kitchen before I went out that maybe the wallet would turn up once I was out of the house. We'd switched the telly off before I left and Mum had told the kids they all had to search the house for the wallet. Maybe it had fallen out of my bag somewhere. Apparently, the children stayed on the couch, but

Mum looked around everywhere. She said that when she was downstairs using my computer later in the evening, before I got back from the gym, she heard a dripping sound. She thought the noise was coming from the laundry next to the downstairs toilet, but then Sammy came down from upstairs. She said she'd been up there to use the toilet. Mum didn't think anything more at the time about Sammy going upstairs rather than using the downstairs bathroom.

At dinner, Sammy assured me that I would find the wallet. 'It'll probably turn up tomorrow, Mummy,' she said. 'When I lose something at school,' she reassured me, 'people say, "Look in front of you." I'd be looking all around and I wouldn't see what was right in front of my nose.' She moved her head in all directions to demonstrate someone looking around everywhere.

That's when my phone rang. I had my fingers crossed hoping it was the bus company ringing to say they'd found my wallet. I'd rung and reported it missing before I left for the gym. But it was Michael the cleaner. It occurred to me as I walked upstairs to my room with the telephone close to my ear that I wouldn't have any money to pay him.

That's when I saw my wallet. There it was on the table next to the bed. The side of my bed that I don't tend to use. Strange that it was there. Had I absent-mindedly placed it on the bedside table when I took my mobile to my room?

I walked back downstairs ecstatic with joy and Mum gave me a big hug of relief. We all went upstairs then so I could show everyone where I'd found the wallet.

'It's funny,' I said. 'I don't usually put things on that side of the bed.'

'Maybe you came upstairs with it,' said Sammy, pretending to re-enact a scene. 'And put it down there. Then you remembered something and went to the other side of the bed.' Sammy acted out the motions of someone putting something down, having a thought, and then going to the other bedside table.

I looked in my wallet. Four fifty-dollar notes. But maybe there had been some smaller notes.

Later, I said to Mum, 'Do you think Sammy did it?'

'We don't know for sure,' she'd said.

'The thought only occurred to me when I realised she'd been in my bag to get the crisps out,' I said to Mum. I put my fingers up to my forehead as if about to shoot myself in the head. 'It's only when I saw the packets in her room that the realisation dawned on me.'

I'd looked around for Sammy's money purse to see how much was in it, but I couldn't find it in her room. That's when I remembered her telling me she's saving up to run away from home. There's no doubt about that girl – her determination to have her own way.

8

Madelaine

I told Sammy we were going to meet my new friend Graeme on Sunday. Graeme and Graeme's son, who is the same age as Sammy.

'Is Graeme your "sort-of" boyfriend?' she'd asked.

How did she know that? I suppose having his photo on my phone is a giveaway. And she saw me talking to him on Skype one time.

'The one with the brown skin and the fuzzy-wuzzy hair?'

I must say that Graeme is a bit of a dude. When we met up with him on the Sunday, he was wearing one of his hats and big dark aviator glasses. His hair stuck out the sides.

'Take those glasses off,' I said. 'Or you'll scare the kids.'

Afterwards, Sammy said that she knows it mightn't happen, but would she call him Daddy? 'And if you have other children, would you still be my mummy?'

I assured both the children that they would always be my children and more important to me than any other children.

Amazing the way that girl's mind works.

9

Out of the clear light of May, with its morning chill that cuts through the children lined up in the playground, distinguishing each child waiting there for the first bell, appeared the angular shape, first the hands, both hands, then the face of Sammy. Her arms reached out, and she wrapped them around me.

I can't say with any certainty when she first spotted me, but I hadn't been there for long. Her hair was flecked with dew in the low morning sun. One or two drops lingered there. Not on her face, pale like parched linen, or her cold moist hands.

I stepped back and kissed the top of her head. Her brown hair unfolded on her neck, delicate as fine porcelain.

She was proportioned like a child. She was dressed like a child.

10

In the school holidays, I open my front door to Sammy on the step. Like any outsider, she is exempt from all the rules: she wears only a dressing gown and slippers, her hair long and matted, a huge teddy bear astride her shoulders. She slips through the doorway grinning, allowing a quick hug.

Hi, darling. Come on in, I say with a half laugh. I look quizzically at her and shake my head. Not dressed?

She sits herself at the dining room table where I've got all the art and craft set up and she begins to draw.

When she's finished she says, This is a one-eyed monster with big lips, a bow in her hair, high heels and funny hands. This one is a fairy blob see, like the other one. These are her fairy wings, her high-heel shoes, her tights, her lips, her big eye. I did this one first and then this one and then this one. A reindeer with horns and a 3D glitter nose. And see this dog? It's like looking through glass. See his paw prints.

11

Lying on a mattress on the floor in the lounge room trying to get to sleep, she shows me how she likes to rest on big teddy's shoulder. I kneel down beside her.

Sammy moves the arm of the bear across her chest so she's in his embrace, like a furry lover.

She tells me it's good with Pat. You know…there's someone to play with us when Dad's busy. And she can paint my nails. And there's another girl in the house. Not all boys. Dad can't paint nails.

The next morning we take the scooters to the park down the road. The one with a concrete path beside a stream.

See the waterfall? Sammy calls out. See there, it goes through there and down there and over there. Did you see the baby eel? He's so cute. He's turning around. Look. Yes, I can draw the eel. Locked in head. Picture of eel locked in head, she says, fingers pointing to her forehead.

13

James's legs have changed visibly. In public, he assumes the aloofness of any other eleven-year-old boy. His school bag on one shoulder, his faded school hat askew. But he can't stay still. He can't stand for very long, waiting for his sister.

When I pick James and Sammy up from school, I wait by the play equipment in the playground, hanging around with the other parents and grandparents, but James, who gets out of class before Sammy, wriggles and rearranges his arms. His knees are muddied and grazed as if his legs are even now in the afternoon light growing, muscling-up, and when he moves his face in hello, his legs and arms seem to elongate. His legs weighed down by his big black shoes. Those legs, those two definitive stabilisers, have hardened, have given him whatever they can of a loosening and a passage through the air, and he goes with their flow.

Other boys, revved up for escape, joke around. But James, whose face seems to inflame and set hard in his neck, sets his legs free, and they break through the atmosphere, where the ligaments and tissues and sinews, where the restless energy of his whole body, is contained.

14

Sammy

It was a shock to find myself on the other side of the front door. I've never seen Mum lose it like that. She's so quiet usually. She shut the door on me. I was in the hallway. The long hallway that leads outside. She probably thought I'd stay there till she let me back in again. But I opened the big front door. Stepped out into the street. I walked up the hill. I was wondering where I would spend the night. I lay down on the grass near the road. My face was very close to the ground. I could see all the ants moving around. It was prickly too. I wouldn't be able to go to sleep. So I got up and walked further up the hill. That's when I saw Mum coming along the street. I hid behind a tree.

Cooee, I called out, hoping she'd find me.

My brother was with her. I'm sure he was feeling sad that I'd gone.

There she is, he called out.

I can't remember what happened after that.

15

Madelaine

Sometimes I've just had enough. Every day this week has been a battle. One morning we arrived twenty minutes late for school. Today she said she's too sick to go, even though she seemed fine yesterday. I had to physically put all her clothes on and carry her down to the car. It nearly killed me.

'I'm going straight to sick bay when we get to school,' she warned me.

After the missing wallet episode, Mum asked me what Sammy had said about saving up to run away from home. I must block things out. I couldn't remember anything she said. I was in tears of frustration and self-pity when I'd arrived at the Mothers' Day lunch. It was the last straw when Sammy wouldn't put her seat belt on to get there. It felt like she was determined to ruin my Mothers' Day.

I started crying as soon as we arrived at the lunch. Mum handed me a tissue and said it wasn't my fault. She said Sammy was born like this. She put her arm around me but I couldn't help myself and pushed her away.

'It is my fault,' I said, shouting at her in frustration. 'I keep giving in. The television. I should get rid of it altogether.' I wiped my eyes and blew my nose. 'I've created a monster,' I said after more tears.

The thing is, Graeme agrees with me. I need to show Sammy who is in control. But I'm not in control. She wins every time. She's so determined. Graeme says he doesn't know about taking on two children – and one of them so difficult.

<h1 style="text-align:center">16</h1>

I realised, whenever Sammy talked, the spaces around her, inside, outside, each person, the plainest thing – iPod, TV remote, eyes, sky – became compacted. Nothing was left to chance. Nothing evaporated. There was much sulking and pleading, and sometimes a determined slamming of a door, the rooms of the house covered with pillows and blankets first here, then there, as a nest was built, room after room, one couch or corner after another, then the outer rim, a solid woven container of sofas.

When we arrived home from school, Sammy ran ahead from the car, up the back stairs, in a direct line from the car park that led to the courtyards, where she waited for me to unlock the door. In the stairwell, we followed the handrail all the way up and then around to the back wooden gate. With one hand, Sammy used the railing to bound up the stairs. I followed behind her.

Shut the gate, she called down to me. Don't let the cats out.

Please help me with the bags, I called up to her. Just take this small bag of shopping.

She came down and took the bag.

When she'd taken up her position on the couch in front of the TV, I said, Mummy told me you bought some new toys with your Christmas money.

She nodded, her eyes on the cartoon.

Can I see them in the ad break? I asked.

She leaned over the couch and lifted a blanket up from the floor. Here they are, she said.

On the floor beside me, she bent her knees and sat down. She lined up the six soft toy animals, all with large black eyes. This is a giraffe, she said, stroking its furry coat. This one is a gorilla. This one a leopard, I think.

Oh, and this one is a cow. And this is a hamster, or it could be a weasel. We don't know. Mum and me aren't sure. And I know all their names, she said proudly. I only got them yesterday.

She turned the animals over on to their stomachs. Their names are on tags, she said. See? But I'll tell you.

Then she flipped the animals on to their backs so we couldn't see their name tags. Romeo, she said. The gorilla. Correct.

She checked the tag attached to each animal as she said its name. Safari, she said. The giraffe. Correct. Speckles. Speckles. Daisy. Daisy. Nibbles. Nibbles. Rebel. Is it a b or a d? She curled one finger in a circle beside an upright finger. Rebel, she said.

She sorted the animals into pairs. I've put them into couples, she said. These two because they've got purple eyes, these two because they're on safari, you know, safari animals, and then these two.

Sammy looked at the television and shook her head, so that her hair flicked out – a brushing away of incidental matters. She laughed her fragile laugh. It bubbled then stopped; it was willing to share her accomplishment, and it said, I am able to read and remember. Against great odds, such a struggle with the letters, it said, I can do it.

In the kitchen I'd cut up a carrot into long thin strips to dip into the small round carton of hummus. I placed the plate beside Sammy on the chair.

She leaned her body forward across the arm of the couch to see the television better, and kept dipping a stick of carrot into the sugar-free snack.

What colour are your glasses? I asked. I've never seen them.

She squinted at the screen. Purple, she said. But I'm fine now. I don't need them. She pushed the plate of food to one side. That's all, she said. I can't eat any more.

I knew what was fitting and legitimate to ask. I'd mastered the protocol, and knew which behaviour, which events, to ignore. Too close to the television. No matter. Choose your fights.

James let himself in the front door and walked over to the couch, across the shag rug, and on to the black leather chair, where Sammy was perched.

How did footy go? I asked.

We won.

Why don't you have a nice hot shower? I said. It's great for sore muscles.

No thanks. Not yet. He sat with his back straight and watched the TV then picked up his iPod, which lay on the back of the couch and placed it on his lap. He logged himself in and pressed the icons.

Did you buy a hot chocolate with the money I gave you? I asked him.

He laughed. My sister's stealing the change out of my pocket.

Sammy jumped up from the couch and ran to the kitchen, where her wallet lay on the bench. She laughed at an unsteady pitch, then grinned at me before putting the coins in her pink wallet.

Here's twenty cents change, James said, digging into his shorts.

Samantha took the other forty cents.

No matter.

17

I thought I could understand why Sammy, having run away once, would want to keep saving money in her wallet. But when I'd asked her why she hadn't spent her Christmas money, had waited so many months before buying the new soft toys, she said, with an impatience in her voice, I don't know why.

One rainy week when I'd picked Sammy and James up from school, and James had gone off to his guitar lesson, I asked Sammy if she did journal writing at school.

The journal? she said. What we did at the weekend?

Yes, I said. I'd really like to read what you write. Can I see it?

We aren't allowed to bring them home. I have to leave it at school.

Maybe everyone will bring their journals home at the end of term.

Sammy didn't answer.

Unpacking their school bags, I kept an eye out for Sammy's journal, but I didn't see it. I did find her glasses case wrapped in a plastic raincoat in the front pouch of her backpack. I looked around the dining table near the kitchen and on the floor beside Madelaine's desk, and I must have sat down, heavily, on the white leather chair beside the couch.

Sammy heard me and looked over, laughing her own laugh. Mum unpacks my school bag, she said. You don't need to do it. Mum will be home soon.

I'd made it a habit when she came for a sleepover at my place in the school holidays, to ask Sammy about her dreams, but she said she didn't have any. She'd still go off to sleep with her iPod playing pop songs into her ears. She told me her password so I could turn the iPod off before I went to bed and before I clicked on my own music.

In the mornings I'd record my dreams. Sometimes I'd read them out to her and she would say, yes, that's weird. Your dreams are so weird, Mummy Two. I wish I had some dreams.

Now I saw half as much of Sammy, since the separation of her parents, I dreamt about her even more. My dreams had become amazingly clear, all the environments and the people within them sharp and precise. In these dreams, I could look into a person's eyes and see the exact hue of their iris, the clear or veined whites of their eyes, and the depth of their pupils, not knowing, though, if I could see everything that was visible. In one dream, Sammy was lying next to me on my pillow and we turned towards each other looking into each other's eyes and I saw her, all that she is, totally, absolutely, in every detail, in all her shades of black, white and grey. It took many minutes of looking to really take in who was in front of me, there was so much to absorb. In another one of my concentrated dreams, I was talking to my daughter, and my own voice, my very old voice, disintegrated into speech bubbles, and then to ripples across a stream, flowing between the banks of a river. The sounds were no longer sounds, but lime-green and moss-green vegetation that contained the body of the pale blue water.

Once, I wanted to mention the nightmare I'd just had – a short truncated dream of Sammy swimming to the opposite bank of a river. But I thought better of saying anything. I remember watching from the side she had come from, her head bobbing up and down as she stroked across the huge expanse of the water, and I saw what she saw waiting by the red muddy edge of the river.

18

It's no good, Sammy said.

She was spreading whipped cream on the pavlova, and I was slicing up strawberries and kiwis.

The sides keep collapsing, she said. It won't hold up. You'd think it would when you take the paper off the sides. It's not as if you can eat that stuff.

She set a row of strawberries on the outer rim of the cake and dribbled extra cream on top. I like decorating, she said, cakes and cookies. Mum and me made meringues again and I did the sprinkles on top.

19

Madelaine

I'd planned the family birthday party for a Friday night and told everyone we'd order pizzas; told them not to come till four-thirty because we had a three o'clock appointment with the school counsellor, and then to the skateboard shop with the birthday boy; tidied up the house on Friday before work; didn't forget to place a Shopfast order; chopped up salad bits for the big glass bowl; asked Mum to bring a pavlova; told my brothers to bring drinks; when everyone asked what to buy James for his birthday, I asked them if they'd like to chip in for a laptop; checked I had birthday candles and a box of matches; told Mum that Sammy likes to decorate the cake; laughed when everyone suggested that Sammy should get a job in a cake shop; borrowed an extra dining room chair from next door; enjoyed the sound of Sammy's laughter. Didn't say to my brother, Stop tickling Sammy, we can't hear ourselves think. Was happy to see her hugging her two uncles. Noticed the holes in her black tights, the whole of one knee exposed. Was pleased Mum had bought her the new pleated voile skirt and the purple jeans and the other assorted tops, including the one with a pussy cat face. Didn't bash myself up about Sammy's hair, so wild and long and unkept it looked as if she had no mother to care for her; was pleased she wore a white singlet beneath the fine fabric of the cat top so her developing body was less obvious. Watched my brother creep his fingers along her back in a playful manner to make her laugh. Tried hard not to feel a rotten mother when Sammy had a meltdown before dinner and I had to go upstairs with her to calm down the screaming. Did my best to explain the behaviour away: it doesn't help that she hasn't eaten anything. She's always like this on a Friday, the weekly Handover Day.

20

Tell me, Madelaine said, what was it that you and Sammy could see on the river bank? And what was it you could see beneath the water?

21

Madelaine

The word is, severe dyslexia – according to the school counsellor. He said her intellect and learning ability don't match. There's no problem with intelligence. But knowing how long the problems at school have gone on for, he apologised for having not met Sammy sooner. Yes, well we've known for a long time she's slightly dyslexic. He said she's got the reading and writing age of a Year One child. It didn't help that last year's teacher was fresh out of college. It must be very hard for Sammy at school. I feel so sorry for her.

22

Madelaine said that Sammy likes to go shopping for clothes. So there were Sammy and me on an expedition to Chatswood, Sammy changing the radio station in the car, bopping her head to the music, talking a little when I'd ask a question: Yes, Mummy Two, Nana bought me a whole pile of new clothes, but I leave them at Dad's. Nana said I need to clean out my wardrobe, things that don't fit and are too old. She's very fussy. Sammy turned to me and gave me a little smile.

There was a sensitivity and a wisdom in Sammy's responses that sometimes surprised me. She was all-seeing but unable to keep up at school. She zoned out. And occupied with the television or her iPod, she seemed unreachable; often she wouldn't respond when I spoke to her, as if she were in a trance, or she'd say, Stop talking. She had the sensitivity of someone convinced she would never be like everyone else.

Usually I couldn't help but think the one worrying thought: she looks so skinny. She has diminished herself, physically, which allows her to fit into small boxes or buckets, or washing baskets, without any effort. Her moods are erratic. Able to sit and eat at the table one day but then unable to stay still the next.

I was the one bearing witness. And like a jury, I weighed up the things I heard and saw.

I was afraid I might discover something inside her that I didn't want to disturb. Or cause her to run away from the world she had constructed. Afraid she would keep her head under the water for too long.

23

During the winter, James grew almost to the same height as me, each month his cheekbones becoming more prominent and his fleshy ears secured closer to the edges of his face. His neat, newly cut hair fell into soft waves above the close-cropped sides of his head. James absorbed conversations, without looking up from his iPod or turning from the computer screen. And his own voice emitted a variety of sounds that rang out from the muscles of his broadening chest. He spoke with authority, and I'd ask his opinion on things: What sort of car do you think is the best value for me to buy? Do I really need to upgrade my mobile phone?

When he left for school on a Friday morning, for the week at his Dad's, his mother kissed him goodbye. And when she picked him up from school the following Friday, the Handover Day, she would sit on the couch between her two children and he'd lay his head on her shoulder.

James's girlfriends at school, if there were girlfriends, would have stroked his hair first, then stroked his hands, I can imagine that.

And when the school term ended, his hair had grown long again. It hung down past his eyebrows, separating on either side of his eyes. His mother kissed him on the head and put her arm around his shoulder.

We have a new plan for Sammy, she told me in the kitchen. She explained that things had got out of hand, completely, and now was the time to do something. The plan concerned a Learning Intensive Course. Sammy would have to go every day to a special program at Macquarie University. But she needed agreement first from Sammy's dad.

After dinner, at the sink in the kitchen, she said, When Sammy gets to high school it will be too late. I'll need all the grandparents to give me a hand with chauffeuring her there and back every day, she said. You're my car pool. The taxis.

The expression, and the way she said it, were full of irony. Bent over the sink, she stifled her laughter, swallowed it down, keeping the sound suppressed. She stopped stacking the dishwasher and straightened up to laugh out loud.

I looked at James and, yes, he'd heard everything. Listened to it all. He'd heard these things before.

Don't look so worried, Mum, my daughter said to me. I know it must be hard for Sammy. I feel so sorry for her.

24

I told my daughter what she wanted to hear, nothing more. That was our way of being together, counterparts, my daughter and the one so delicately balanced. Sammy used up her mother's patience, in her erratic and demanding mood swings. Daily challenges wore away at her mother's confidence. She and I, both foils, kept our opinions to ourselves and let our encouragement renew Sammy, as if it was within our capabilities to support her enough, and our words of praise sustain her. It was the relentless amount of patience required, the speaking softly when wanting to scream with frustration, the getting her dressed, the attempts to get food into her stomach.

I keep telling Sammy, my daughter said. That's the thing. If only she'd get it that she'll feel better if she eats something.

Tell me about last week, I said. How did things go?

Well, you know, Mum, she's always been immature for her age. But I want to know. What was it you saw in the dream?

25

The dream: Sammy swims overarm from one river bank towards the other shore. She jumps, not from the side, not from anywhere, straight into the rippling water, into the murky blue, streaked with darkness, but her jump proceeds, uninterrupted; she plummets down and scatters the sunlit waves that hang off her, and then open up to receive her, beading along her arms and along the strands of her hair. She sees the muddy outline of the crocodile basking on the bank of the river.

And I see the crocodile too. A female guarding her crèche. And that is the dream of the dream: me seeing what Sammy can see. As she swims closer, the sun's silver rays scatter behind her; and in front of her. Sammy positions herself towards the bank and heads in. At the last moment, by one stroke of her arm, the water parts, separates, a whirlpool of water on her right swirling downward with a strength at odds with the potency of her plunge. The whirlpool splits at its edges, and inside, it spins and ensnares itself with a cylinder of empty space. Even with the speed of the current around it, the whirlpool does not slow down in its spinning, but gathers momentum and thickens. The swirling water rotates around itself without losing power, gyrating, and in the same moment, Sammy, almost at the shore, is able to breathe underwater and plunges down.

She drops into the well of the whirlpool and she sees to the bottom of it whatever is there. She keeps her eyes open, for the whole long fall of the downward spiral.

By bending her knees up tight into her body, empowering her jump, Sammy speeds her drop but not enough to blind her to the shapes and pictures reflected in the water. What else is there to see? The river is full of crocodiles. There are mothers and their babies, close to their crèches, crocodiles basking close to the sandbank.

Sammy flashes by and the line of water throws out images until they begin to fade and disintegrate, an album of connected pictures, many pages of drawings, but each one the same size, and the images moving like a cartoon as the pages flick past and then spin around in the water and float there, but not ruined and not blurred.

See the reflections on the water, says Sammy. She is speaking to me.

We overtake dozens of pictures. The lighter the shallows of the river, the narrower the cylinder of the vortex.

Sammy lifts her arms, and stretches, then points her fingers, bends at the elbow, one at a time. Here, her arms are both thin, identical in fragility, and her movements make her body twist on to her side in the water, as she reaches one arm in front of her and then the other. I watch her powering through the river. Her body speeds up. With neat kicks of her feet, her toes fan out like flippers.

We may be outside the swirling water; I don't know any more where we are. Sammy's arms and lips blur blue with the colours of the river. Her body elongates as smooth as a seal's. And there I am, over there, a person just like me, waist-deep in the river, water dripping from my hair. And then Sammy disappears beneath the surface.

26

Sammy lay along the length of the couch in front of the TV, as if adrift at sea, marooned on the ocean. Rolled up in a thick blanket all the way to the top of her head, positioned on her stomach, only her face visible. When I went over to say hello, she pulled her head in all the way, like a snail retreating into its shell. Within the roll of the blanket, her hiding place, her face was obscured, except for the black hollow of her cocoon. Her feet were stretched out and resting on her brother's lap. Her hair was matted, fluffed around her head, so that the strands, almost as dark as the black leather couch, fell down past her shoulders. I knew she was in an uncommunicative mood. On the other hand, she flashed me a brief half-smile before withdrawing back into her cocoon when I tried to approach.

Madelaine and I hugged hello. Madelaine, dressed and ready for work.

James and Sammy, transfixed, were dug in, directly in front of the screen, James on his laptop, and me waiting for the show to end so I could say, Turn it off, we're going out into the sunshine. Now. Turn it off now, that's enough screen time. Now, you heard me, okay, now, get yourselves dressed and we'll go to the park.

They ignored me.

But at lunchtime, we had sandwiches sitting on the trampoline out the back in the sun.

Well, one person ate sandwiches, said James when I told Madelaine.

Sammy ate nothing, I said. I feel bad that they watched so much TV.

You could have been firmer with them, she said.

They don't do what I tell them.

They will if you're firm enough.

I offered to take them to the park, I said. But they didn't want to go anywhere.

They just wanted to stay home and veg out, she said. The last day of the school holidays.

And so I drive to Redleaf Pool as I often do, and sit down at the café, under the tin roof where I can see the harbour. The water laps the shore, ferries cross the water, I rest my chin in my hands and berate myself.

Severe dyslexia. Does it help to have a diagnosis? I'd asked Madelaine when she'd told me the results of all the tests.

No, she'd said. Sammy's still difficult. She hasn't got ADHD, though. So that's something. They say we need to reinforce what she's able to do, not what she can't do. Apparently, according to one of the specialists, Sammy and I are in a dance together.

27

The clouds across the sky were puffy and grey. Close against the side window of the car Sammy had pressed herself into the back of the seat. The netball game had been due to start in fifteen minutes. Sammy still needed to have her hair tied back to participate in the game.

Back home again, Madelaine and I stood in the courtyard outside her door. It was a cool day and we'd left Sammy downstairs crying in the car in the garage, while James played on his skateboard. By then, the netball game would have started – without Sammy.

When we got out of the car, Madelaine had told Sammy she could stay in the car and think about what she'd just done.

Madelaine told Sammy that Coach would have spent an hour working out everyone's positions. And he had you down to play shooter, she said. And Grandma has come all this way to see you play.

Stop saying that, screamed Sammy at her mother, her face still covered up by her tracksuit top that she'd draped over head for the drive back home from the netball courts. It makes me more sad, she cried.

Madelaine beckoned me to follow her up the steps and away from the children. We were both struggling to control ourselves, to stop from opening the floodgates to our own tears of disappointment at the way things had turned out.

In desperation, I asked my daughter, What did all the psychologists and doctors say? What did they tell you about handling these situations?

Madelaine raised her shoulders up around her neck with frustration. They diagnosed extreme determination and stubbornness, she said. They told me it's hard when she's a child, but they'll be great character traits when she's an adult.

That's not much help. And the last doctor? The specialist paediatrician?

When we saw him in his surgery, Sammy just sat there in the chair being the perfect child. The thing is, no one knows what she's like unless they live with her.

Madelaine looked off into the trees. The branches were bare of leaves and the trunks a faded grey.

It's so upsetting, she said. People don't know what it's like. One of the mothers at the netball said – people don't know how hurtful it is when they say things – she said that apparently the week-on and week-off arrangement with her dad isn't so good for children.

It's good for you, though, I said. You've told me you wouldn't be able to cope if you had Sammy the whole time.

Madelaine wiped the tears from her cheeks. People don't realise how upsetting it is when they say things like that, she said. It's not perfect, but better than what it was before. I tell them she's always been like this. Even before the split. Anything can set Sammy off. I don't know what it was. Maybe because I said in the car that she hadn't competed for five weeks. They were due to play the A team for the first time this morning. Maybe that's what upset her.

Is there anything I can do to help? I asked my daughter.

Have you got a gun? she said.

28

Here you are, Sammy, I say. Look, there's Nefertiti, whose name means 'the beautiful woman has come'. Here she is with one of her daughters. Look, there's Bastet, the cat goddess, a daughter of the sun god. She's a woman with a cat's head. As a mother goddess, she's often seen with kittens. See the kittens at her feet? Did you know that pet cats sometimes sat under the chairs of their owners at feasts? But they were more often out hunting in the marshes with their owners. The pet cat wasn't just a mice catcher, it was also a hunter and a killer of the snakes that frightened the Egyptians. Cats could be trained, as a trusty retriever expected to bring back birds knocked down by the toss of a stick by its master. Isn't that amazing?

That's awesome, Sammy says.

29

Madelaine

Even in my car, with the moonlight flaring in on top of my head like a burst of glitter, I can tell how they arrange themselves in the dining room on the wooden chairs, the five of them, Graeme, Aiden, Mum, my son and my daughter. The moon slants in through the sun roof, a silvery circle in the sky, light so bright that everything else in the car becomes dim; and because the moonlight keeps coming in and darkening the grey interior, my thoughts focus on the scene at home where the five sit under the bright rings of the down lights. My friend Graeme (just a friend, not a boyfriend) will have taken his place at the head of the table, his Manly Sea Eagles cap turned backwards. My daughter, Sammy, refers to him as Graeme-with-the-fuzzy-wuzzy-hair. He's attentive to all the children, not just his son Aiden, who is Sammy's age. My son, James, either taps the keyboard on the computer at the desk beside the table, or leans back in his chair on the other side of Aiden, as they discuss the result of the grand final. Sammy is listening. Mum is in the kitchen.

Graeme had rung in the afternoon to see if he could come over. When I told him I was going out with the girls and Mum was babysitting, I said he was welcome to stay on and have dinner with Mum and the kids. I knew he'd say yes. He's not one to knock back a free meal. I heard Graeme ask Mum if she'd had a good day. Funny how he said he didn't want to meet any of my friends or family – apart from the kids. From his experience, he reckons they've all got an opinion on things. But there he was making conversation with my mother.

I remember the sounds of the banter and laughter around the dining room table.

At the end of the meal, Sammy made dessert for everyone. There wasn't much in the fridge or in the cupboard so she climbed up on the bench, then straddled the hotplates to search all the usual hiding places for some treats to put together for dessert. All she could come up with were three marshmallows. So she got some powdered drinking chocolate, melted huge spoonfuls of it with water – Mum trying to limit the amount of chocolate, unsuccessfully of course – and, after placing each marshmallow in a large white bowl, she drizzled the homemade chocolate sauce on top. It all looked very professional.

See how well-behaved Sammy is in front of Graeme and Aiden. She knows how to be a good girl. I've seen her trying really hard. I said to Mum, What I'm worried about is when she's a teenager. Drugs and all that.

Mum said it's the same with all kids and that Sammy isn't 'bad', just difficult.

Sometimes, when things are really difficult, when she has one of her meltdowns, screams non-stop, and even shakes with rage – that's a new thing, the shaking with rage – I think that maybe it would be best if she went to live at her father's full time.

Sammy's father keeps saying that I must be lazy because the homework doesn't get done the week she's with me. He's still telling me what a terrible mother I am and that he doesn't really want to have the children every second week, but he doesn't want me to have them – you and your mother, was what he said.

According to James, when they're with him, Sammy does her homework and her reading every night. But it hasn't always been like that – only since Pat's been living there. Sammy doesn't want to misbehave in front of Pat. She's caused me a lot of pain, that woman, my old school friend.

The psychologist, the one who specialises in dyslexia, said a day at school for Sammy is like running a marathon. She said that expecting Sammy to do homework on top of coping with a school day is very hard.

It's so hurtful, the whole situation, my ex living with my old friend,

Pat – all happy families. James told me they even have a games night once a week. When Sammy's with me, it's chaos the whole time. She's worked out how to plug the TV back in when I disconnect it, because I've threatened no television until the homework gets done. Five different plugs she has to reconnect and she does it. Every time I lose a fight with her, the next battle is harder to win. She uses it to gain ground until she takes control again.

I feel such a failure.

I imagine the sound of their laughter, the rise and fall of it, raucous then muted. And then the laughter gags, like a woman choking. I try to get help but can't turn the key in the lock because of the torn ligaments in my hands, still from the ski accident. I can't get back in the front door of my own house. The door is shut tight, and the frustrations and achievements contained in the house, all of their reverberations, have already receded, far far away, until they vanish altogether.

I should turn round and drive back home and light all the candles. But the car is on automatic and I can't reverse. Anyway, they are all there together, the five of them. From downstairs, Sammy would have to walk up to her bedroom in the dark, and then hop into bed and under the covers. The laughter rises in pitch. Sammy is laughing along with them.

Later, when I give her a kiss goodnight, she opens her eyes and whispers, Mummy what's the matter? Mummy, what is it? Are you still dizzy from the accident?

30

Today, at Rose Bay, at low tide, I walked out on the sand bar through misty rain. I didn't know which one of us to feel sorry for the most – I couldn't decide. I thought I would walk there and think about Sammy, her brother, their mother, and me. But wind pushed into the mist, and nothing remained visible or solid – not the mud crabs, not the men and women out there throwing sticks into the water for their dogs, and not even the sounds remained attached, voices saying Get it boy, come here, come back, now. So, I thought, feel sorry for nobody. I returned to my desk and finished this work.

Here, I'll show it to Sammy and tell her it's a story about lotus blossoms. I worked away in my office, reminding myself, it doesn't matter if she can't understand. But she'll know that the blue water lily closed at night and reopened in the day. I'll tell her the Egyptians believed it was linked to the sun god, who disappeared at night and was reborn at dawn, and I'll show her the drawing of the lotus blossom shutting its flowers at night and withdrawing so far into the water that it couldn't be reached by hand. And, there, I'll say, at day break, leaning to the east, the lotus blossom struggled upwards again to open in the light. The lotus emerging from the water, the symbol of the sun breaking forth from the darkness.

31

Such a small café, a row of round tables, supported by chrome legs, a counter and black bar stools, all of the facades sleek enough to deflect stripes of daylight and send them away as feathered dust. The walls rough, a patchwork of recycled crate panels. On the concrete floor, James rocked his chair, back and forth, front legs to back legs, bang-bang, so slow the sound distorted to a down to earth thump-thump.

A rock band played a medley on the radio. It was a treat for Sammy and James to be devouring ice creams. I sat with my sun visor in my lap and licked on an ice cream, too.

I'd driven their mother to the top of the hill and she'd said to me, Do you know what James asked? He asked if there's anything in my life I regret. No, I said. Apart from going over that ski jump. That's the only thing I regret.

Dressed for work, her big leather handbag over her shoulder and a bottle of water in her hand, Madelaine strode to the bus stop.

I watched my daughter hurry away, one arm swinging the bottle forward and back, and then I walked with Sammy and James to the café.

Sammy licked the chocolate ice cream from around her mouth and listened to the thumping of her brother's chair. I watched her eyes looking out through the window and down the street where the road dropped away at the corner, down toward a park. Dogs chased sticks on the grass at the bottom of a gully. The road rose to the west, visible as it rounded the corner and tilted upward before turning sharply, up towards the fire station.

I followed Sammy's eyes, but how could I know what she saw? The diamond-flecked pavement? The pub across the street? Or, at the sharp twist of the road, did she see that Alsatian whose long saliva-covered tongue sagged between razor-sharp teeth? Something coming out of the bushes. A figure in action. That far away, with the position of the avenue of trees, the shape came into sight, then out of sight. Somebody is rushing to get on a bus? To get away?

Madelaine liked to go places. I like to get away on a bus or a train or a plane, she said. I've been thinking, maybe the children should live with their father all the time.

A police car passed on the road, and James stopped banging the chair legs and looked around the café. His eyes followed the row of tables to the chrome sugar containers and then up to the radio. He crossed his arms on the table top. What station do you think the radio is on? he asked Sammy. He smiled, his chin crinkling into a dimple.

From her pocket, Sammy pulled out a tube of dried pasta. She'd threaded a strand of purple wool through it. She listened a moment. Nova, she said.

James traced his finger around the patterns of sun on the table top. Correct, he said.

Sammy took a deep breath before blowing through the rigid tunnel of the pasta. A whistle, she said. She stood, and blew again.

The strand of wool was going places. It escaped into the air like a runaway streamer.

<h1 style="text-align:center">32</h1>

It was Sammy's idea: a visit to the school's sick bay. She said she was burning up. A Monday – one of those after-school special-reading-class Mondays. More reading was the last thing she felt like doing after a day in class, and it was up to me to get her there.

On the way to school that morning, she'd told her mother that she wasn't feeling well.

I left Sammy screaming at the bus stop, her mother said to me, but at least she walked there – with a wobbly walk – but she didn't sit on the pavement and refuse to budge. Poor James. I felt dreadful leaving him with Sammy carrying on like that. But she would have stopped the tantrum…in front of all the people on the bus. Do you think she was really sick? Madelaine asked.

I said, It's hard to tell with Sammy.

Sammy came out of the sick bay just after the going-home bell. She said she'd only been in there a few minutes, and then the bell went off. She reckoned Luke and Charlie said that her arms were red and so was her face. So she'd put her hand up and told the teacher.

She'd come towards me in the playground, her eyes half closed, her mouth turned downward, and handed me her backpack. Her maroon and white chequered school dress moved in the wind and attracted attention to her feet, to her ankles. She wore black cotton tights and bright pink ankle boots with a zip up the back. In her boots, she looked more steady than James, whose shoes had worn through at the front and his big toe, covered in a green sock, hung out as he flapped toward me in the playground.

I carried Sammy's school bag as we walked to the parking area adjacent to the shops. James said he'd go and buy takeaway milkshakes for the two of them.

We'll wait in the car, I said as I handed him the money.

I held the door open while Sammy climbed in. She pulled out a Smartie cookie from the paper bag I'd left on the seat, letting the crumbs fall on to her dress. Her fingernails glowed a luminous lime in the faint light inside the car.

James won't be long, I told her. I hope he sees where we're parked.

There he is, she said. He's seen us.

James walked over to the car sipping his drink. He passed a milkshake through the window to Sammy. She frowned and said she'd wanted a big one.

It is a big one, he said. See, the container's round and thick.

I held their drinks while they clicked on their seat belts and then sat there in the driver's seat for a moment and listened. There was some noise from the parking area. Being in the middle of it all, the car doors banged against my head, like the noise of a chef chopping in a kitchen, rat tat tat. And there was the noise of milk and froth being sucked up through plastic straws.

I thought about their mother at her desk in the city. I just want to be a grandmother, I'd said to her. And do grandmother things.

The whole thing, everywhere, all over the place, everything, continued as before.

33

It was a battle to get Sammy to the after-school reading class. She was ashamed, ashamed to be seen entering or leaving Maryanne's special lessons held in her office at the back of her home. Maryanne Beggs, Reading Psychology – Dyslexia specialist. A line of palm trees grew at the front of the house, their browned and splayed fronds sweeping towards the grey slate roof tiles. A closely cropped lawn faced the long driveway where a brick wall led to the side door of Maryanne's study. Sammy would hide behind a tree or a shrub until the child before her had left and was completely out of sight.

I could see the door of Maryanne's office from the car where I waited for the lesson to finish: the sky a smoky grey, bunched-up and irregular in texture. But the longer I waited, the more blue sky emerged, a container for the scene, a tiny corner of hope. I could see one thing, and then I could see a little more.

The afternoon air was humid, with a dampness hanging low over the road. The air of the suburban street, the air of the brick wall and the driveway, enveloped me like a sticky web.

In the car, I stretched out my arms. The steering wheel was still warm from the heat, the long November day, and I leaned back, as if it were somehow the beginning of a new day, and I shut my eyes. Cars passed on the road, accelerating with a belch once through the pedestrian crossing, then rumbling off. The sound diminished as they rounded the corner.

On the other side of the doorway, I could imagine Sammy, just as her mother had described how it was when she insisted Mummy stay with her.

At the end of the lesson, when Maryanne opened the box of treats-for-good-work, Sammy smiled her fake smile of appreciation, but when

120

Maryanne turned away, Sammy rolled her eyes at her mother. She didn't think much of the trinkets in the box. And then, outside, Sammy pretended to bang her head against the brick wall in frustration, just like her father.

The afternoon smelled of jacarandas, and white magnolias. The aroma carried along the street, off the nature strip and across the road, between the trunks of the trees, and in through the window of the car, where the scent merged with the smell of the empty gingerbread-man wrapper on the seat – a heady sweet smell.

In the past – how long ago? – when I was with the family, the seasons came one after the other, always predictable, the browning of the leaves, the unfolding of the spring blossoms, death and regrowth, falling then opening in perfect timing. And we swept it all up and fooled around, enjoying ourselves. A child's game. We all played along. We didn't realise it would end. Nobody did.

These days, I might say to my daughter, How was your week?

Good, she'll say and look across at me. If Sammy hasn't driven me to tears, it's been a good week.

On the way home, the traffic was bumper to bumper, a stop-start flow. Each set of lights seemed to take an eternity to change.

Back at the house, Madelaine said to James, How about a hot chocolate? She poured a glass of milk for Sammy. The tin of powdered chocolate high up in the cupboard was on a shelf where a person would not be able to get at it easily, to pull it down and help themselves. Madelaine reached up.

From the desk in the adjoining room, James called out, No thanks.

Madelaine lifted the stainless steel kettle and set two coffee mugs on the bench for her and me. I apologised to James as soon as I got home, she said, for leaving him at the bus stop this morning with Sammy screaming. I told him I felt dreadful.

I lowered my voice so James couldn't hear and said, He slammed his bedroom door on me again today. I'd told him he had to make a start on his homework before computer time – Mummy said. His eyes filled with tears and he stamped up to his room and slammed the door. Oh no, not again, I thought. It had taken me four days to get over last time when he refused to speak to me for the rest of the day. We hadn't bought him the new pair of shoes because Sammy was playing up at the shopping centre. I'm just following instructions, I called out as he stomped upstairs. I'm just the grandma, I said to his back. It's not my fault, I said. He'd shut the door with a bang.

Madelaine cleared her throat. He's probably still upset about this morning, she said. Calm down, Mum. It's okay – a bad day. The other two days were good. Two good days and one bad one. Don't forget to say the same thing to me when I have a bad day. She glanced into the other room.

James had his eyes on the computer screen on the desk, absorbing its addictive familiarity. He'd declined the hot chocolate from his mother the way a person can knock back what is offered, every time if necessary, with the intoxicating power of being in control, and, I could imagine, with another sense of power as well, the stomach-churning taste of acceptance as the mind writes out on its head: this is my sister, this is the way she is. This is the way it is.

I needed to learn it too. This is the way things are.

35

Madelaine

In my painting, the camels are now in sharper focus, with woven saddlebags over their humps; the blur, the initial blur of paint, had no clarity at all – washes of colour, on a large canvas, my latest work-in-progress. Then the pyramids rose from the landscape, triangular shapes on the horizon, the camels gradually becoming more defined. Very distinct. They evolved out of the dust of the desert, and the pyramids appeared and blue sky came through.

The camels take up a third of the space of the canvas now. Their shapes emerged from the paint – their humps, the desert, the pyramids. The three camels, one behind the other, were moving forward. Very slowly. That's all there is to it.

But the thing is, Sammy could see the figures of the camels before anyone else. That's the point, Mum. The point is Sammy said Egypt as soon as she saw the early wash of colours. Pyramids. She can see images in clouds or in formations of colour. That's why she's so good at drawing. Da Vinci, Picasso, Rodin. I tried to tell her about all the famous people who are dyslexic and to read her the story about the girl who wanted to be a great artist. How the girl tries and tries, really hard, to be like someone with dyslexia so she can be a famous painter. But Sammy wouldn't listen. She won't have a bar of it.

Sammy was so proud up on stage today. A Most Improved Award from the remedial teacher. Sammy said the prize was for being top of the dunces. She said that, or something like it: how she got first prize for being the number-one-dunce.

36

Sammy watches a wildlife show instead of cartoons. It's not time for *Big Brother* yet. She's astonished as a male crocodile emerges from the mangrove swamp and lunges at a female croc. Sammy takes a deep breath at the same time as her mother and tells her, or tells me, See, see that crocodile?

James sits at the desk and does his homework, and Sammy calls out, Come and watch this, James.

She lies back on the couch against her mother, wriggles closer. They gasp together as the crocodile attacks.

Madelaine's face is smooth, no laughter lines set into an arrangement of marks – no lines spanning out from the sides of her mouth or from the corners of her eyes. She holds her face in its established pattern. She has adopted Sammy's television preferences, having given up on her own viewing habits, and now her eyes too, watch through the commercials and glance up only when a person enters the room. She's a captive to Sammy's moods.

Come here, James, Sammy calls again.

He's busy, Madelaine says. Is the TV too loud, James?

We have to write a book, he says. Twenty pages. The assignment says to write a children's book and do all the drawings.

Sammy could do the illustrations, I say.

No. I have to do it.

What are you going to write? his mother asks.

James spoons vanilla custard into his mouth, straight from the carton. It's about a dog, he says. The dog's master throws a stick and the stick lands in the back of a truck. The dog jumps in to get the stick, but the truck takes off for Perth. The story is the dog finding his way back home.

Great idea, says Madelaine. You just write your story, James. We'll be quiet over here.

Sure, Sammy says, and snuggles in and butts at her mother's chest, like a baby wanting to feed, and squints. Just write your book, she calls out to her brother.

37

After the school holidays, when the flood waters in Queensland had receded and the fires in Tasmania were under control, Sammy and James started the new school year. I remembered the previous start of the year, when Sammy was eight and a half, when she'd said to her mother, Tell them at school that I've been hit by a bus and I'm dead.

Getting her out the door in the mornings was always a battle. I've been dreading when they go back, said Madelaine. Sammy doesn't want to move off the couch – so much anxiety about school.

Even Sammy's father said he'd had a tough time with her, that second week of first term. So I offered to come over to Madelaine's the following Saturday and take Sammy out for a swim. James would be at cricket. But as soon as I knocked on the door that hot and humid afternoon, Madelaine hurried me into the kitchen.

She spoke in a hushed voice. The thing is, Mum, she said, pointing out through the glass back door, Sammy's tantrums have become more dramatic. Look what she's done. She totally lost it yesterday because I said she couldn't watch TV until she made a start on her homework. A meltdown. A two-hour tantrum. Shaking with rage, she threatened to stab me and to set the house on fire. At one stage, I had to lock her out till she calmed down. I don't know what the neighbours thought with all the screaming. She was shouting out, My own mother. My own mother does this to me. Then she went round to the back and trashed the place.

I looked out to the backyard, saw the overturned trampoline, the school bags still lying out on the grass, bits and pieces flung everywhere.

You won't want to hear this, Mum, said Madelaine, but after that, she self-harmed.

Oh no, I said, struggling to keep my voice normal. You've got to do something.

She started to hit herself with a branch. I let her back in, but then this morning she came downstairs and said, I don't want us to keep on fighting. How about you do what I want.

In the next room, Sammy was beating out a rhythm with a stick, up and down a scale, tapping first a glass bowl, then the wooden table, then a box of coloured pencils. I walked in to say hello, noticing the dark grey under her eyes, and the paleness of her face. She was wearing her new torn-off and frayed yellow denim shorts; fluorescent tangerine sandals. She didn't push me away when I put my arms around her.

I haven't forgotten the rules, I said, No kissing.

There are times when, in the same room with Sammy, I can sense her determination, whole slabs of it, as deadly as a firearm. She stood up and turned on the TV. I picked up her school journal and tried to look at it beside her. Madelaine had told me that the school diary finally made it home at the end of the year and I'd asked if I could see it.

First, I looked closely at the cover with its brightly coloured-in shapes. I like the cover design, I said to Sammy.

Someone must have put some water on it, she said, pointing to a small smudge of colour.

I told her how much I loved the drawing that showed her diving beneath a big wave and swimming under the sea.

She nodded.

I looked at the 'what I did at the weekend' stories: friends she visited, Luna Park, family birthday celebrations, what she ate, her brother going to sport, her own game of netball, a ski holiday, staying for two days with grandma.

And Fathers' Day: I wanted to make Daddy breakfast in bed but he was in a rush to go to the rugby.

The journal is great, Sammy, I said, closing the book and putting it back on the table. Well done! Would you like to go for a swim when Mummy and James go to cricket?

Her head moved slightly in the affirmative.

Madelaine hurried towards the door with James, who was all dressed up in his cricket whites. Are you sure you don't want to come with us to the game? she said to Sammy.

Sammy frowned and shook her head then stretched out on her stomach on the couch. That's when my phone beeped and there was a text from May Ling and Alexander's dad to say it was okay for us to come over for a swim. I sent a message back, We'll be there soon.

Let's get going, sweetheart, I said picking up her black and white bikini and scrunching it into my handbag. I've told your cousins that we're on our way.

In a minute, she said, taking her time to get off the couch. Slowly, she rolled on to the floor, next to the cat on the rug, then lovingly patted Mister Sphinx on his head. Then a good scratch under his chin. Finally, out the front door and down the steep stairs to the underground parking area.

Come on, darling, I said as she completed circuit after circuit of the driveway on her new two-wheeler. Let's get going.

She kept on riding.

And then there was the problem of where to leave the bike while we were out.

Someone might steal it, she said, alarmed.

I didn't have a key for the garage and the bike wouldn't fit in the car. Sammy insisted we try squashing the bike in. First into the back seat and then the boot. We lifted it up and put it in handlebars first and then back wheel first, but it was too big. I had to go through the motions of trying to get her bike in the car. A meltdown loomed, signalled by a high-pitched urgency in her voice. And it was all my fault. My back ached from all the lifting and shoving. We'd emptied my boot and I was parked across the main driveway into the parking area. If someone drove in, we'd be blocking the entry with the contents of the car strewn across the concrete.

Let's put the bike in the house, I suggested.

But, no, she was determined the bicycle would make it into the car – somehow.

When she acted up on me like this, with her frustration turning to anger, and with no way around the stand-off, that's when I felt the tears of helplessness well up in the back of my eyes, gather up and fall down my cheeks, very quietly. Out of control. I lifted the body of the bike, the bright pink glitter frame with the streamers hanging from the handlebars, a bicycle designed for trick riding; moving slowly and carefully, and with a prayer on behalf of my arthritic spine, I carried the heavy bike back up the stairs and locked it inside the house.

A silent car trip to May Ling and Alexander's house and the swimming pool. I clicked the radio on to her favourite music station. She wound the window down and looked out. A shift in the afternoon light, from the solid interior of the car to the glare of the sun reflecting on the glass of the high-rise buildings. Birds, cicadas, crickets, the sea in the distance, the waves, the sand, the sea gulls and the thirsty biting of flies.

I've got the air con on, darling, I said. Aren't you hot? The car will stay cooler if you wind the window up.

She ignored me.

Her uncle smiled in greeting when he opened his front door. Where's my hug? he said to Sammy, his arms wide.

She ran up and wrapped herself around him.

38

I go downstairs to the kitchen to look for a plastic straw for Sammy, and one for Alexander. They want to use them as pipes to blow water at each other in the bath. They're still wearing their swimming costumes after their games in the pool. In the bathroom, they fill the bath while tipping buckets of water over their heads. They've said they'll turn the taps off when the water level is high enough, and they won't let it overflow. I find two straws, one bright orange, the other lime green, and hurry back upstairs. The tiles are slippery from all the splashing.

While the children play in the bath, May Ling collects bottles of nail polish from the bedroom. She lines the colours up beside the sink, ready to paint Sammy's toenails.

My back aches. I lie on the floor in the hallway to stretch out my spine. Through the door I can see them and hear their laughter as Sammy and Alexander pretend to smoke the straws like cigarettes.

May Ling jokes in a voice like a school teacher, Stop it, Alexander. You know you're not allowed to smoke tobacco.

She's a tall girl for thirteen, and she leans down over the bath and reaches for the taps; she folds herself almost in half to turn off the water. Sammy and Alexander had fun with her in the pool. It involved pushing them over the edge with a straw broom and then they'd climb out and then she'd push them back in again.

Sammy stands up in the bath, and out of the bright afternoon circle of light, she stretches a leg over the porcelain. She looks very thin and one-dimensional, a figure diminished by immersion in water; May Ling reaches out a hand to help her, hoists her cousin over the ledge and leans over again, pushing the plastic buckets to the side.

May Ling says to Sammy, When you get changed, we'll do your toenails.

Sammy goes through the door into the adjacent bedroom, while May Ling and I pick up the rest of the bath toys. She leans forward so that her hair falls into the white bubbles. Alexander climbs out. My feet, bare on the tiles, are cold, and my head, near the pane of the window, is warmed by the glass.

Outside, within reach of the sun's light, I can make out the shape of my daughter's legs, walking away from the front door. She's wearing her city stockings, the shiny ones, and shoes with stiletto heels. Her skirt and top must be light too, because they reflect the sun, and she passes like a photograph of someone running, the legs blurred.

I open the window. Usually my daughter waves and calls out. But now, when she does not, I follow her arm, a shallow shadow, until I see her hand rigid at her side, as she walks.

She's holding a large canvas suitcase. She moves like a person weighted down, leaning towards the bag. A shadow falls across the canvas; another long shadow is pulling at her feet.

Wait here, I say to May Ling.

Outside, I give my eyes time to adapt. Madelaine does not walk very fast, and I won't have trouble catching up. The afternoon changes, slowly, from a painting full of colour, to an empty canvas; emptiness, clouds drifting across, and then they fade away. The row of fig trees opens up ahead to the road. Finally, the sky is simply grey, a blanket of precipitation.

Madelaine is halfway along the avenue, moving away. Her heels clack, steel on stone. Keeping my head down, my eyes straining at the uneven surface in the dappled light, I push forward walking as fast as I can. The pavement is littered with red berries from the trees overhead and the seeds break and roll away where I step. I'm clearing a trail. The air is humid, so I undo the buttons of my cardigan. Before too long, I'm jogging, my jacket flapping, all over the place, with each stride, but I'm jogging, and my daughter is slowing down.

At the end of the row of trees, she stops and puts the suitcase down.

Where are you off to? I call.

Oh! she says. And she slumps, lowering herself on to the bag. So it's you, she says. What's the matter?

That's a big suitcase.

What? I've picked up some hand-me-downs from May Ling.

Such a big bag?

Big? Madelaine looks at the suitcase on the ground, under her body. She nods and laughs a breathless sound. Oh, she says. So it is. She nods some more, and reaches for the handle with her ski-damaged hands, her fingers unable to curl all the way around the strap.

I help my daughter up, and she stands for a moment, looking all about. She reaches up to the top of her head and releases the clip that keeps her hair in a twist and lets her curls fall all around her face and on to her shoulders. She takes a long blonde lock and pushes it behind her ear and then sweeps it all across to one shoulder.

Her face has a new angle etched into it, and I feel uneasy as the setting sun makes its way behind an apartment block and the sky darkens. She turns and looks away from me, and I see only the back of her, her hair swept unevenly to the side. Her shoulders are set squarely under the linen shirt; they are level but constricted, as if she has tucked her blouse in too tightly at the waist, too constraining. The lightness of her shirt darkens in the darkening of the air, and she appears to be part of the change – a natural progression that moves a person from one place to another, passing under an avenue of trees. Her legs, in the shiny stockings, glow as if iridescent. Her feet, attached to orange leather shoes, are elevated from the pavement. When she walks away from me, her stilettos carry her. Her head is positioned in one direction.

39

She walked further under the trees. Not far away, she stopped.

Where she stopped, there was no blue visible. No space between the clouds. And she leaned to the side and put the suitcase down. The closest patch of sky was where I stood, but what could I do or say that would change anything? The house was beyond the yawning chasm, an immense gap between sky and earth. And the clouds, all of the earth's clouds, were too far away to reach.

In the middle of the path, I yelled towards my daughter, Madelaine!

I thought for a moment my yelling had parted the leaves that connected the trees, that thick canopy overhead. Rain had started to fall, and the grey sky had lightened, moving east to west, and the drops had fallen through the air, and the atmosphere had been cleansed by the water, until my daughter had been forced to turn around. With her shoes kicked off, she would have already broken into a run, abandoned the bag, and headed for home.

Part Four

Mothers need a break from mothering. I'll start with that, if anyone asks. You know how it is, I'll say.

The bench beside the sink in the bathroom is long and narrow. Sammy sits up there, her back against the mirror. May Ling is bent over her, painting Sammy's toe nails. She has coloured each of Sammy's big toenails a shiny black and the others a brilliant blue.

Is everything okay? I ask.

Sammy gives me the thumbs-up sign.

I lean over her feet, beside May Ling, and, willing my hands to steady themselves, I use a cotton bud dipped in white nail polish to draw a smiley face on each of her black-painted toenails.

Sammy looks down and grins at the two of us working at her feet. I'm the King, she says proudly. No, I'm not, she corrects herself. I'm the Queen.

Queen Hatshepsut, I say.

I'll tell Sammy about the great Pharaoh Hatshepsut, the only She-King of Egypt. I'll show her the murals on the walls of Hatshepsut's terraced temple, mention her fleet of five wooden ships on an expedition from the Red Sea to the Land of Punt. Look, I'll say, see the thirty rowers on each boat, side by side, slicing through the River Nile, each stroke moving them closer to Punt, and there – look – there is the homecoming: the potted myrrh saplings, sacks of frankincense, fragrant ointments, wood, ebony and ivory, all collected on the journey and brought back home. If Sammy wants to know more, I'll tell her the details.

The great Hatshepsut, I'll say. Egypt's most determined Queen.